ONE EYE LAUGHING, THE OTHER WEEPING

THE DIARY OF JULIE WEISS

BY BARRY DENENBERG

Scholastic Inc. New York

PART ONE

VIENNA, AUSTRIA
1938

SUNDAY, JANUARY 2, 1938

Daddy came home very late *again* last night. It may be a holiday for everyone else in Vienna, but not for Daddy.

I kept reading and reading, trying to stay awake (I simply *cannot* go to sleep until I *know* that Daddy is home), hoping that at any moment I would hear the elevator doors open and close with their clash and clang, footsteps echoing in the hollow hallway, and the sound of his key sliding slowly into the door lock.

But I must have dozed off because the next thing I knew I could smell his eau de cologne and he was giving me my good-night kiss. Daddy *never, ever* goes to bed without giving me my good-night kiss.

Daddy sees more patients each year, which means he sees less of *me* each year. I wish it wasn't so but Daddy is simply devoted to his patients.

He doesn't even come home for his noontime meal like he used to. When I was little he *always, always* did unless, of course, someone had an emergency. Milli says when I was little I insisted on standing out on the front balcony until I saw Daddy coming home.

Milli would make sure everything was ready — Daddy didn't have time to waste because he had to rush off to his afternoon house calls and then return to the office by three, where he would always find a crowded waiting room.

He liked to eat quietly and not have to talk because it was his only break from the tedious pressure of worrying about his patients. I would just sit there silently, watching him eat.

They all call him "The Doctor." Not "doctor" or "Doctor Weiss," just "The Doctor," with a capital T, as if for them there is no other.

Milli says I used to tell anyone who would listen that if they went to my father they would *never, ever* get sick (which made Daddy laugh every time he heard it. Daddy is pretty serious most of the time and it's hard to make him laugh. I'm the only one who can. He calls me his precious jewel. That's because of my name, Julie).

At least the night before last he was home on time. We all drank a toast to my birthday and the New Year (they're both on the *same exact day*). It was my first sip of champagne and I don't see why everyone makes such a fuss about it.

Mother didn't drink *any*, not even to make the toast. She never drinks *anything* — not wine or champagne, even on special occasions like this. She said it makes her too nervous.

Daddy always makes the toast, but this year all he said was that he wished everyone a healthy New Year, which was pretty brief for him (usually he's much more eloquent than that).

Daddy gave me the diary I am writing in at this very moment and the silver-plated fountain pen I'm using. He wrote on the card: *Because I know you have so much to say.* The diary is covered with a bright red silky material and there's a ribbon so I can keep my place. Of course it was not exactly a surprise. I saw it at Heller's Book and Stationery Store weeks ago and have been hinting ever since.

But the pen *was* a surprise — it came in its own little case and rests on a little velvet bed with a gold band that holds it gently in place. It's my first *very own* fountain pen. When I'm finished writing I'll carefully put my new fountain pen back in its case.

Mother gave me a small silver locket but she didn't

put anything in it because she thought it might be nice if I decided for myself what that should be.

Max gave me a book of Rilke's poems because that's his favorite poet. Inside he wrote:

> To my sister, Julie:
>
> "Nearby is the country they call life.
> You will know it by its seriousness.
>
> Give me your hand."

Sometimes I can recognize my brother by his seriousness, although I must say it is a beautiful book.

The problem with Max is that he thinks he's smarter than everyone. He even thinks he's smarter than me just because he skipped the third grade and I didn't, which was only because I didn't want to. (If I wanted to I could have.)

He's eighteen and goes to Vienna University. Max is *very* serious, as I said, and *very* ambitious: He wants to be a famous lawyer someday.

I'm glad he's on crutches. I'm *glad* he broke his leg skiing in the Alps. He thinks he's the best at everything.

Milli made my two favorite birthday desserts: coconut cookies and almond-paste coffee cake. Plus her annual birthday present: gold-wrapped chocolate coins, one for each year.

MONDAY, JANUARY 3, 1938

Milli played solitaire while I told her how badly Max has been behaving lately. She's usually playing solitaire when I come home from school, and I have to say that sometimes I think she plays solitaire *all day long*. (She says she likes it because it's something she can do on her own and it helps her not to think — which wouldn't appeal to me in the *slightest* — why would anyone want to play something that helped them not to think? I like to think.)

Since he's been attending the university Max acts like he's a thousand years old. I've started calling him Maestro Max, which he clearly dislikes (I'm delighted to say).

He used to be more likable. We used to talk a lot — he loved to help me with my problems, you could tell. He always knew the *exact right* thing to say, like that time last year when Sophy and I had that horrible fight because she couldn't stop laughing after I had my hair cut very short. It wasn't the least bit funny because up to then my hair had *never* been cut and was almost down to my waist. I just felt like I needed a drastic change and all my best friend could do was laugh.

Now he has a sign up that says NON INTROITUS, which means "No Entry" in Latin. Of course I don't pay any attention and just go right in, same as I always did. I told him I don't speak Latin.

Milli didn't get a chance to tell me what she thought about all this because Mother was pressing the buzzer and Milli had to go see what she wanted.

Milli's the only one of the staff who Mother *really* trusts. She's the only one who's allowed to dust the paintings in the living room that are Mother's pride and joy.

Mother rules the staff with an iron hand — sometimes she spends all morning going over the chores. Each and every one of them is afraid of her, except for Milli.

Mother gets *very* upset if everything doesn't go precisely as planned and right now everything is *not* going precisely as planned.

For one thing, she's working herself into a state

planning her annual dinner party. This year there will be eighteen guests — four more than last year. Milli said Mother wants to move to a bigger apartment because our dining room is so small since it only seats twenty comfortably. I'm not sure if Mother's joking, or Milli is, or both.

Mother has only herself to blame for the mess she's in. If she hadn't fired the cook she wouldn't be in such a panic.

Milli says Mother is *absolutely* certain the cook is the one who stole the cigarette case Daddy gave her for their twentieth anniversary. She fired the cook before this one because her shoes squeaked and Mother said it was giving her a migraine headache.

I don't think the new cook is going to last long. For one thing she's much too pretty. Mother doesn't like to hire anyone who's pretty. "Too many complications," is the way she put it once, when she didn't think I was listening. I think that means boyfriends coming around. Maybe that's why Milli's been with us for so long. She's been here from the time Max was born.

Milli's pretty much on the plain side. She looks just like an owl — an owl with glasses. She even blinks slowly like an owl. I think everybody looks like some kind of animal. Daddy, for instance, he looks just like a llama. Mother's like a canary and Uncle Daniel is a double for a rhinoceros.

Milli never, ever goes out on a date or gets a call. She never goes away on holiday and even in the summer she comes with us to Bad Ischl.

I think she doesn't like to spend money because she's saving up for something, only I don't know what it is.

For a while I think Richard was interested but she hardly *ever* speaks to him because he's just a chauffeur. (She can be that way.)

Mother has already sent out the invitations, even though the dinner is six weeks away. According to Mother, that is not nearly enough time to get everything properly organized. I think that's why she decided to hire the pretty cook — she can start right away.

And the cook isn't the only one Mother is upset with. This is the third morning this month that the milkman has left the wrong order and the washing and ironing hasn't been done yet so I can't wear my new yellow dress to lunch, which is Mother's absolute favorite of my new dresses.

TUESDAY, JANUARY 4, 1938

I've tried to talk to Milli two nights in a row now but she's been busy showing the new cook where everything is and how Mother likes everything done.

Mother's dinner party has everyone on edge (as usual), and Milli's trying to make sure everyone's doing precisely what they're supposed to.

I decided to talk to Milli while she was taking her bath. That's the only place I can ever be assured of any real privacy with her.

Milli said that when I was a baby she would take me in the bath with her and that's why I like to be there. Sometimes I sit on the edge of the tub, pull up my dress, and dangle my feet in the water. Other times I just sit on the floor next to the bidet, which I used to think was for washing your feet, but I know better now.

Milli's the cleanest person I know: She takes a bath *every single* night. Even when she's working around the house she smells like lavender. That's because she keeps little sachets in every single one of her dresser drawers.

Lavender's my favorite scent in the *whole wide*

world — except, of course, for the eau de cologne Mr. Pisk puts on Daddy after he shaves him in the morning.

I think the reason Milli talked about when I was a baby is because she'd rather I didn't come in while she's taking a bath anymore. Maybe it's just as well because lately I've been distracted by Milli's rather enormous bosoms that are right there, bobbing up and down on the surface like they were alive.

I sure hope mine don't get that big. I've been keeping an eye on them lately and frankly I don't think I have much to worry about, although you never know about things like this. It's entirely possible to go to bed one night a perfectly normal girl and to wake up in the morning with enormous bosoms.

I told her what Max did yesterday, how he started locking his door now *even when he's not in his room*. Milli listened very patiently — that's one of the things I really like about her. Most adults *pretend* to listen, but don't really. Milli and Daddy are the only two exceptions I can think of. Maybe Mrs. Thompson, too.

Milli said that, perhaps, I should consider respecting Max's privacy more, which seemed like a pretty foolish thing to say because I don't respect his privacy any *less* than I used to, so why is he acting so strangely now?

But Milli didn't answer that question. She just said it wasn't a good time for me. By that she means the astrology. Milli is guided by the heavens. She doesn't take a sip of water without consulting the position of the planets.

According to Milli I'm a Capricorn. She says since Max is a Cancer we're a square to each other, which means we don't get along so well (which isn't exactly news to me and doesn't make any sense because Daddy's birthday is the *same exact* day as Max's and I *always* get along with Daddy.) Milli's a Gemini, whatever that means.

I handed Milli one of her fluffy white towels as she stepped out of the tub. I tried not to look at her bosoms.

We had to go through the kitchen to get to Milli's room, which is quite small and there's only one little window that hardly lets in any light (it's so high up you can't look out it and anyway, it doesn't matter because it only overlooks the inner courtyard so there's not much to see even if you could see out).

Sometimes I sit in bed with her while she looks

through her giant astrology book that's filled with lots of funny drawings and symbols that tell about the planets, their position in the sky, and what it's all supposed to mean.

It's really curious that Milli believes in astrology because she's so down-to-earth when it comes to everything else. Frankly I think it's all a big bunch of nonsense but I make believe I'm listening so Milli doesn't feel insulted. I'm quite a good actress when I want to be and, besides, I don't mind listening to her talk about it because she makes it sound so magical and mysterious I'd almost like to believe it's true.

It's like you can read people's minds or see the future. I used to think it would be the most wonderful thing in the world to be able to see into the future, but lately I'm not so sure.

Mother thinks Milli is "too clairvoyant for her own good." (I heard her saying that to Daddy one night.) I didn't know at the time what clairvoyant meant but I do now and I don't know how anyone can be *too* clairvoyant for their own good.

And, besides, I like being in Milli's room because all my things are there. She has every one of my dolls since

I was born including Doo Doo and Habe Sabe, my doll kitchen and tea service, teddy bears, rocking horse, and my favorite books: *Ferdinand*, *A Little Princess*, *Dr. Doolittle* — so I really feel at home when I'm there.

THURSDAY, JANUARY 6, 1938

Max's problem is that he's too charming for his own good. He thinks he has everyone fooled, although I must admit he's sure got Mother wrapped around his little finger. She believes everything he says, no matter how far-fetched it is.

I didn't speak one word to him at dinner tonight, but of course that isn't unusual because speaking at meals isn't exactly encouraged at our house. Mother believes children should be seen but not heard — especially when a meal is being served.

Daddy and Mother always sit at opposite ends of the long dining room table while Max and I sit in the middle of either side while Milli serves.

Mostly we just sit there while Mother regales Daddy, in excruciatingly boring detail, of her activities of the day: where she shopped and what she bought, where she had lunch and whom with. Plus she reviewed all the plans for the party: who's coming and who's not; what's being served, when, and on which china.

Daddy nods at the appropriate times, shakes his head occasionally, sips his wine, and says, "Is that so, Anna," every now and again.

Sometimes I wonder why they married each other in the first place. I know you're not supposed to think things like that but I can't help it.

They're opposite in every way.

Daddy chooses his words with the utmost care while Mother chatters away about the most trivial things: bridge, the theater, problems with the servants. Daddy spends most of his time reading and worrying about his patients while Mother spends half her life doing crossword puzzles and the other half shopping and socializing. Mother is *seriously* concerned about being fashionable: She is *forever* looking for the latest dresses, the finest furs, and the most exquisite jewelry, while Daddy wears the same blue suit every day (even though he has other really nice ones hanging in his closet).

Mother likes to go out and Daddy likes to stay in. He doesn't even go to the coffeehouses like Uncle

Daniel. Mother tries to get him to go to parties, the theater, or their box at the opera, but even when he reluctantly agrees, something always seems to come up at the last minute with one of his patients and Daddy promises to get there as soon as he can.

Of course Mother *is* beautiful, I must admit, and Daddy does like to see her looking pretty.

FRIDAY, JANUARY 7, 1938

Sometimes I can't believe the things Max makes himself for breakfast. This morning he cut two thick slices of black bread, slathered butter on one, cream cheese on the other, cut a piece of last night's ham that was just as thick as the bread (honest), and ate it standing up, talking about Rilke all the while.

I told him the reason he talks so much is because he's making up for lost time. According to family legend (which can't always be relied on) Max didn't utter a sound until he was six, which is a real shame. I would so much have preferred a mute for a brother.

MONDAY, JANUARY 10, 1938

Ernst Resch tried to look up my skirt today at recess. That's the second time this week. He thinks he's *so* sly I'd never notice him standing there even though *all* the boys were on the other side and he was the only boy on our side. When I asked him if he was lost, his face turned tomato red and he started to stutter so badly I couldn't for the life of me understand what he was saying. He decided to go back and join his gang who were playing marbles, which is pretty much the only thing they know how to play.

He's such a bully. If you don't watch out he'll try to trip you or spill over your inkwell. Each year he gets even worse although he stays away from me most of the time — I think it's because he has a crush on me.

Even though he's so annoying sometimes, I feel sorry for him because of what happened to his twin brother (who was stung by an insect when he was four and died from blood poisoning the very next morning).

I told Milli about how Ernst tried to look up my skirt but now I'm sorry I did — she wasn't very understanding.

She says I spend too much time "dwelling" on things like that, although I'm not one hundred percent sure what she means by "things like that" (and the way she says "dwelling" you would think it was the *absolute worst* thing a person could ever do in their life).

She says it's because I have so many planets in Libra. "Too much Libra for such a little girl," she says, and then makes a little clicking sound with her tongue. I *adore* it when Milli makes that clicking sound, although *she* denies that she makes any sound *at all*, clicking or otherwise, and whenever I say something about it she says I should have The Doctor examine my ears.

(Frankly I think she's still upset with me because I won't let her walk me to the streetcar anymore in the morning. I'm old enough now. I'm in seventh grade already.)

Milli promised if I finished *all* my homework we could play double solitaire so I came right home after my dreadful piano lesson, went directly to my room, and finished all of it by dinnertime.

I *adore* playing double solitaire with Milli. We both play really, really seriously, slamming each card down onto the table and laughing so hard sometimes we actually fall off the bed.

WEDNESDAY, JANUARY 12, 1938

Mr. Pisk didn't come to shave Daddy till seven-thirty this morning, just as I was leaving for school.

"Running a little late," he said, sounding for all the world like the White Rabbit in *Alice's Adventures in Wonderland*. Now that I think about it, he looks just like a rabbit with that protruding pouty face of his and his eternally twitching nose.

Usually he's come and gone by the time I'm even up because Daddy likes to be in the office no later than eight. (Daddy's always the first one up. Mr. Pisk comes at seven, gives him his shave, and Daddy leaves right after that so I only see him for the briefest moment every morning.)

Mr. Pisk didn't want to talk to me but I insisted. I told him he simply *had* to do something about Daddy's hair, which looks just as disheveled after Mr. Pisk cuts it as before. He said it was Daddy's fault and I asked him how that could be since *he* is the barber and Mr. Pisk said that if Daddy would just comb his hair, perhaps it wouldn't look so frightful all the time. He has a point but still there's no excuse.

I don't know why Daddy puts up with him. Daddy

admits he doesn't do a very good job because he concentrates more on telling stories about the old days than he does on cutting hair.

Just last week Daddy asked him if it was cold outside and Mr. Pisk told him a long story about the winter of '28 when the Danube was so frozen you could drive your car over it.

Every time Mr. Pisk is late I don't get to smell Daddy's eau de cologne. I *adore* that smell — it's *so* heavenly and the scent hovers over him all day like a perfumed cloud.

Mrs. Pisk stays at the Steinhof now with all the other crazy people and Daddy says Mr. Pisk drove her there.

FRIDAY, JANUARY 14, 1938

I HATE going to Mrs. Konig's for my piano lesson. I don't know which I hate more: Mrs. Konig, the piano lessons, or her horrible white poodle that never, ever leaves her lap (except, I would imagine, to you-know-what) and starts barking the moment I arrive and doesn't stop until I leave while Mrs. Konig coos lamely the whole time, "There, there, Bella Luna, it's only little

Julie come for her piano lessons." I HATE it when she calls me "little Julie" and I HATE the dog's ridiculous name, Bella Luna. The dog isn't *bella* at all but it sure is *luna*. I can hardly stand looking at her. She has black gums and the hair on her face is stained this horrible orange-brown color because something's forever dripping down from her eyes.

I wish I didn't have to take piano lessons. I LOATHE playing the piano. For one thing I have no talent at all — NONE, and no matter how long I sit there poking at the keys I'm never going to *make it sound anything but awful*.

And that's not all — there's another reason.

Max.

Max is a piano-playing prodigy — he was playing Schubert's Impromptus when he was eight. Whenever I practiced at home — which I don't do anymore — he would make me move over and show me how to play the piece as easily as if he were tying his shoe — which drove me absolutely mad.

By the time Max was ten he could play Schubert's Sonata in D Major. Mother wanted to send him to the conservatory but Max wouldn't go. He wanted to be a lawyer, even back then.

Watching Max play the piano is like seeing a great magician: No matter how closely you watch you just don't know how he does it. His hands hang suspended weightlessly in midair, then glide gracefully and effortlessly over the keyboard — like an ice-skater alone on a frozen pond, his eyes half closed, head tilted heavenward as if the score were up there and not right in front of him (although, of course, he doesn't look at the score because he's such a show-off).

Once I heard Mother tell Max he played just like Aunt Clara, which was startling because no one *ever*, *ever* mentions Aunt Clara, especially not Mother.

Aunt Clara is Mother's younger sister and they had some kind of huge, catastrophic argument around the time I was born and she and Uncle Martin moved to America right after and nobody's heard from them since.

Max says there used to be a photograph of her and Uncle Martin on the table next to the couch in the living room but it's not there anymore. He says she looks just like Mother.

I once tried to explain to Mother why I didn't want to take piano lessons but (as I feared) it was truly a waste of time.

"A proper girl has to have a proper education and playing the piano is part of a proper education," she said with a great air of finality.

MONDAY, JANUARY 17, 1938

Daddy says I should have more friends but I find that most of the kids my age are pretty boring, except for Sophy. She's my best friend — she's also my *only* friend, which is why Daddy said that.

Sophy's *never* boring. And besides, Daddy has only one friend, Mr. Heller, so he's not one to talk.

Sophy has to wear a brace on her left leg because she had polio when she was two. Sometimes when we're in my room and we're sure no one is going to come in, she takes off her brace and lets me walk around in it so I can see what it's like but then, after a while, it gets too scary and I have to take it off. I think it makes Sophy happy to see how scared it makes me.

Sophy doesn't let her brace stop her from doing anything. She's the fastest rope climber in the whole school and a very good volleyball player, too. She takes off her brace when she climbs but not when she plays volleyball.

Sophy's a lot better at sports than I am. I *hate* sports of any kind. For one thing I don't like competition, and for another, I don't like to rush around all over the place getting sweaty and banging into people.

There's another thing that Sophy is better at than me — as a matter of fact she's the best in the whole entire school: drawing.

Sophy's pictures always look so real and everyone else's look so flat and dull. Last week we worked on landscapes and of course everyone drew the same stupid house and the same stupid tree. Only Sophy's looked like *something*. Her tree looked alive. You could almost see the branches swaying in the breeze.

I think she didn't want to play because she's still mad at me. We argue a lot of the time, even though we've been best friends since we were born only three days apart in the *same exact* hospital.

Last week we argued because I got a better grade on my composition.

For as long as I can remember, I have been getting better grades than Sophy and she's been getting mad about it. She says I don't even try and that I was born smart and it's not fair. Frankly, it's getting a little tiresome.

I told her either she could study harder or I could study even less than she thinks I do, which didn't even make her smile, let alone laugh. I'm not even sure she knew I was trying to be funny.

Sophy doesn't have a very good sense of humor.

This time we argued because Sophy finally admitted that she had a crush on Bernard Goldberg, which I found impossible to comprehend and told her so. That's what started the fight. She got mad because I said I knew she was dumb but I didn't know she was blind. She actually thinks Bernard Goldberg is handsome. (She doesn't take criticism too well. She gets touchy about the smallest things.)

She's convinced Bernard B. Goldberg is THE ONE FOR HER.

"He's the one I'm destined to be with, Julie." She actually *says* things like this. She thinks there's only one TRULY RIGHT PERSON for every individual in the world and the most important thing in life is to find *that* person.

She says I'm never going to find my TRULY RIGHT PERSON because I don't try enough, which she is right about because the truth is I just think boys are more trouble than they're worth.

All Sophy thinks about lately is boys, boys, boys. It's her favorite topic. She reads one love story after another, which is where she gets most of her silly ideas.

When she's not thinking about boys she's worrying if she's pretty enough, and no matter how many times I assure her that she is, she still worries.

She says she wishes she were tall and blond like I am. Sophy *is* on the small side, I'll say that, but she has thick, wavy black hair that's every bit as nice as mine, almost.

WEDNESDAY, JANUARY 19, 1938

Yesterday I had to go to the basement of our school and borrow a book from the lending library for my geometry project.

I HATE borrowing books from the library. I don't like being compelled to return them by a certain, specified time. If you can't read a book when you want, what's the point?

That's precisely what I *adore* about books. They wait there, silently and patiently, until the exact moment *you* decide to open them.

All last night I imagined I could hear the book loudly

ticking away as I tossed and turned, vainly trying to go to sleep.

TICK, TOCK, TICK, TOCK, READ ME NOW, OR TAKE ME BACK.

The ticking got so loud I had to go downstairs and put the book in the hall closet.

Besides, once I've read a book I don't want to give it back. It's mine and I want to keep it and place it on my bookshelf right next to the last book I read.

I LOVE to read. Sometimes, especially when I'm trying to stay awake so I can be up when Daddy comes home, I fall asleep right while I'm reading, and then, when Daddy wakes me up, my finger is still in the book saving my place.

Sometimes Daddy scolds at me for reading so late at night. He says there isn't enough light and I'm going to strain my eyes.

Someday I'm going to have a library just like Daddy's, only not with all those medical books that have those horrid pictures in them.

Daddy's read everything there is to read, and he's very proud of his library.

He keeps the books in his library in really, really strict order.

Daddy doesn't mind if I take one of his books to read as long as I put it back in the right place, which I always do. I especially like looking at the books Daddy keeps in the glass bookcase — those are his favorites.

Sometimes when I'm in Daddy's library I lie down on his long leather couch, close my eyes, and imagine I'm one of the characters in a book.

Sometimes I even do it while I'm in school, especially if it's a particularly boring day. I walk around secretly pretending to be a character in a book I'm reading.

Lately I've been Alice in Wonderland. Sometimes I pretend I'm so small no one can see me and sometimes I pretend I'm so tall that I have to be careful not to step on anyone.

I don't like to read the books we're assigned in school. I prefer to read the books I find in Daddy's library or in Mr. Heller's shop.

Mr. Heller has a little bell that is attached to the top of the front door so he can hear when someone comes in. I like to open the door really, really slowly so that the bell hardly makes a sound. Then it takes a while for Mr. Heller to realize someone's come in. Sometimes when I do that he's nowhere to be seen, and then suddenly he pops up from under a table or in between the aisles and starts running around excitedly, showing me all the new books that he thinks I might like (all the while making notes of things missing in this little notebook he *always* carries in his shirt pocket).

Mr. Heller *always* wears a white shirt with a black cloth sleeve protecting it from the dust and a green eyeshade shielding him from the light.

He has a sign over the cash register that says:

YOU CAN'T GET RICH SELLING BOOKS, ONLY READING BOOKS.

All the books are downstairs and the stationery is upstairs. Mr. Heller has every book you could *ever* imagine and if he doesn't have the book you want he gets very upset, like he's committed some unpardonable sin, and he promises to get it for you "momentarily," as if it will just appear if you have faith and stand there long enough.

I like to look at the stationery, too. There are all different types of notebooks, some with colored papers, which are my favorites, and mile-high piles of snow-white writing paper, erasers, glues, chalks, and crayons of every color in the rainbow.

I think the reason Mr. Heller likes to see me so

much, besides that he and Daddy are such good friends, is because his daughter Irene died two years ago. She was eighteen. There was nothing Daddy could do. He went to Mr. Heller's house *every* morning, without fail, for months and months. When Irene had to go into the hospital he was there every evening. He never missed a single day, not even Saturday or Sunday. If he and Mother were going to the theater or a party he would insist they stop there on the way.

I used to go with him on Friday nights, and Mr. Heller was right, it was a miracle the way her eyes would brighten when Daddy walked in the room.

But it wasn't enough. When she finally succumbed Daddy was *so* devastated — I've never seen anyone that sad.

She used to work at the store and she loved talking about all the customers — especially the mean ones. She swore me to secrecy, but then, if I promised, she would tell me all the foolish books they bought and, after they left, we would laugh until our eyes watered.

I liked talking to her. She was one of those real honest people you meet from time to time if you're lucky. The kind who will tell you what they truly think and not just what they think you want to hear.

Mrs. Heller has rheumatic fever, which leaves her constantly short of breath. She always walks Mr. Heller to the bookstore in the morning and then returns to fetch him at the end of the day. They look very, very sweet walking arm in arm like they do.

THURSDAY, JANUARY 20, 1938

Sophy's homeroom teacher, Mr. Erickson, is the strictest teacher in the *whole entire school*. He makes everyone sit silently until he arrives each morning. Sophy says it's really eerie because no one utters a sound, fearing that he might walk in at any moment.

When he finally does arrive he climbs up on this big raised platform where his desk is perched so he can look down on everyone. He looks like a mouse with beady little eyes that are always darting about nervously.

Sophy said he's been really mean to her this year. He said her penmanship needs work and if her long division doesn't improve, he'll have to have a conference with her parents. Sophy started to protest this harsh treatment, but Mr. Erickson said if she continued to talk back to him, he would put her in "the dungeon" where she could spend the rest of the day alone.

She thinks Mr. Erickson is being mean to her because she's Jewish, which seems a little far-fetched to me. Mrs. Thompson isn't mean to me and I'm Jewish, too. But Sophy says that's because she's Mrs. Thompson and not Mr. Erickson.

FRIDAY, JANUARY 21, 1938

I passed the new cook on my way to Mr. Heller's. She said hello, otherwise I would not have recognized her in a million years. She didn't have on her black uniform or white cap or anything — as a matter of fact, she was rather elegantly dressed and looked even prettier than when I first saw her.

Sophy thinks she saw her brother the other day. She wasn't completely one hundred percent sure so she didn't say anything or scream out, and besides she was with her parents so she was afraid to.

Sophy is forbidden to talk about him because her parents had to place a notice in the paper declaring that they wouldn't be responsible for any of his debts. He's not a very reliable person and besides, that's not even all. Her parents are also mad because they caught him necking with his girlfriend.

That's about when he moved out and Sophy hasn't seen or heard from him since.

Sophy wanted to go ice-skating after school today but I couldn't go because of my tiresome piano lessons.

SUNDAY, JANUARY 23, 1938

I spent all of yesterday shopping with Mother. I wish we could take the streetcar instead of having Richard drive us. Driving is *so* boring and the streetcar would be more fun but Mother *never* takes a streetcar *anywhere*.

She says it's because they're always packed (she does have a point — sometimes it's so crowded that some of the men hold on for dear life while hanging halfway out the door). But I think she wouldn't take it even if there was only one other person on board.

We paraded up and down Kärtnerstrasse. Mother bounces from shop to shop like a honeybee buzzing from flower to flower, pointing to this or that, ordering around the quivering clerks, demanding that everything be sent home, including the bill, because Mother never, ever carries money (she thinks it's vulgar).

We went to all her favorite shops: the milliner,

then the furrier, the watchmaker, the jeweler, and Zwiebeck's for a handbag and gloves.

Actually, the shopping part wasn't as bad as I thought it would be.

The only two things I minded were going to the florist to choose the flowers for her dinner party (which took endless hours of deliberation before she finally settled on blue hyacinths), and to Mrs. Svoboda, the dressmaker (which also took forever and seemed even longer because I was nearly fainting from hunger the whole time).

Fortunately we had lunch at the Reiss Bar, which is where, according to Mother, *all* the stylish people go. *I* like it because it's close to Mrs. Svoboda's (it's on a side street right off of Kärtnerstrasse) and because they have very cute little tables and chairs that are covered in pretty red leather.

I don't know why Mother insists on these Saturday excursions because it's really a terrific bore for both of us. I think it's her way of showing me she's interested in my life. But I know she isn't really.

She always asks me the same three things in the *same exact* order: 1) How's school? 2) How's Sophy? and 3) Why do you argue with your brother so much lately? and as soon as I start to answer, her eyes immediately begin scanning the restaurant in hopes of recognizing someone she can then wave to and reel over to their table so she doesn't have to talk to me.

I don't even mind *that* so much, but what I *do* mind is that as part of this obligatory outing, she gives me advice on some aspect of my behavior that I should improve. Last month it was not caring for my nails properly and yesterday it was spending too much time with my "nose stuck in a book" and how I should be more outgoing because "you don't learn everything there is to learn about life from books."

Fortunately the lecture was abbreviated because Mother was getting a migraine. Mother is absolutely *plagued* by migraines. Sometimes her migraines are *so* bad that she has Milli unplug the telephone, draw the curtains until her room is *totally* dark, and bring in a cold cloth for her eyes. Then she just lies there until dinnertime and sometimes doesn't even come out *then* and just rings the bell on her bedside table so Milli knows to bring in her dinner.

Daddy's given her lots of pills for her migraines but I don't think they do any good. I think Mother's migraines are the reason she and Daddy have two bedrooms.

After Richard drove Mother home we went back to Demel Konditorei on the Kohlmarkt for some pastries. They make the best *Mannerschnitten* and *Schaumrollen* in Vienna. There's always whipped cream spilling out of either end, which is how you know if it's good.

When I got home, Mother was resting and Milli said to be sure not to make any noise. Mother hates to be awakened when she's recovering from a migraine.

TUESDAY, JANUARY 25, 1938

I wish I didn't have to wear braces. I'm the only one in the *whole entire school* who does and I look like I tried to crash through a fence. I don't know why teeth can't just grow in like they're supposed to.

All the kids look at me because having braces means you're rich. I know some of the girls talk about how many different outfits I have and how much they cost. I've heard them and so has Sophy.

We *are* rich, at least I think we are, but Daddy didn't even have to pay for my braces because he takes care of Dr. Hirsch's family for free and so the braces don't cost us anything.

And, besides, Mother plays bridge with Mrs. Hirsch,

although I think she's more interested in complaining about the tiny little sandwiches Mrs. Hirsch serves than in actually playing bridge. Mother says Mrs. Hirsch is cheap.

Dr. Hirsch said that when my braces come off I will be so beautiful that I can have my pick of any boy in Vienna. I asked him what second prize was and he laughed and said I had a sense of humor just like The Doctor.

Mother says that Mrs. Hirsch is making a big mistake not getting rid of her cat. Mrs. Hirsch is going to have a baby in a couple of months, and Mother believes that if an infant looks too much at an animal when she's first born she will grow up to look just like that animal.

WEDNESDAY, JANUARY 26, 1938

Sophy got mad at me today because I told her that she monopolizes every conversation, which she does, or at least most of them. Then, just to get even, she said that I dream too much, not the kind of dreams you have at night, but that I'm dreaming too much during the day and that someday I'm going to have to wake up.

For one thing, I don't think it's even true that I'm too dreamy, and even if it is true, I don't know that I'll have to wake up someday, as Sophy puts it. Sometimes she says the first thing that comes into her head without giving it any thought.

THURSDAY, JANUARY 27, 1938

Daddy took me with him to the office because there was no school today. I ADORE going to the office with Daddy, although it makes me sad to see all those sick people just sitting there, waiting for Daddy to make them better.

I once asked him if he liked having all those people depend on him and he said sometimes he did and sometimes he didn't.

It was a very exciting day because as soon as we got there, Daddy had an emergency. A policeman had been accidentally injured in a traffic accident — he broke his arm and was cut very badly above the eye and Daddy had to tend to him right away.

He put his arm in a cast and stitched up the cut, which had been bleeding profusely but wasn't as bad as it looked at first. The policeman was worried about his eye. He was afraid he had lost his sight but Daddy assured him the cut was above the eye — not on it — and that he would be all right. The policeman was relieved and told Daddy he didn't know how he would ever repay him.

Daddy ordered lunch from Kugler's on Kohlmarkt. They have *everything* and they're Daddy's favorite. Only he knows I don't like to go there because of all the creepy lobsters they have crawling all over themselves in that aquarium that is far too small.

Daddy says I didn't like to go to Kugler's even when I was very little, before I could even talk.

We ate lunch right on Daddy's desk — just cleared *everything* off and put a tablecloth down. Daddy had his usual, veal cutlet and cucumber salad, and I had my usual, Sachertorte.

Unfortunately after lunch we had to go to his tobacco shop on Florianigasse, although I didn't go in. I never go in there because the man who owns it is mean and blind. Daddy said he was blinded in the war and that's why he's so mean, but I don't care why he's mean, he just scares me.

Also he has this big, vicious black-and-tan dog that

has a wire muzzle clamped down around his large snout, which makes him look even more ferocious than he already does. Daddy says he protects the store from robbers, but I just wish Daddy would get his tobacco someplace else.

On the way home Daddy had to stop off and visit one of his patients in the hospital. One turned into three and we didn't get home until well after dinner. Mother was already in her room with the door closed. Max graced us with his presence and ate some cake while Daddy and I made ourselves sandwiches. I was watching Max eat and I don't know why but all of a sudden it came to me. He's been acting strangely lately because he has a girlfriend. And, of course, he's keeping it a big secret from everyone. I don't have any evidence or anything like that, but it makes perfect sense. I'm going to talk it over with Sophy and see what she thinks. She's good at this kind of thing.

FRIDAY, JANUARY 28, 1938

It was so cold today I ran up the stairs as soon as I got home from my piano lesson. I didn't even bother to wait for the slowpoke elevators. As soon as I got in I huddled next to the big stove before I even took off my hat and mittens.

You have to stand right next to it because the heat just doesn't reach very far. I didn't budge until I was toasted all over.

SATURDAY, JANUARY 29, 1938

Max has been teaching himself to roll Turkish cigarettes lately. He says it's more "cosmopolitan" if you roll your own. I'm not sure what's cosmopolitan about it but it sure is fun watching all the tobacco end up in his lap or on the floor.

I think his wanting to be cosmopolitan has to do with this new secret girlfriend. Rolling the cigarettes isn't the only reason I suspect he has a girlfriend. Recently he's increased his exercise routine, although I must admit that Max has always been a great athlete. He still takes fencing lessons three times a week and plays for Hakoah, the Zionist soccer team. Max is a Zionist and so are his friends. They wear the Star of David around their necks and believe that all Jews should leave the country they are living in and move to

Palestine so they can form a Jewish state. I don't even know where Palestine is. All I know is it's something Max and Daddy argue about all the time.

Now he does exercises *every* night before bed. I went by his room very, very slowly so I could hear him grunting and groaning and on the way I passed Daddy's study.

I could hear him talking on the phone. It sounded like he was talking to Uncle Daniel because they were talking about Hitler. That's all they seem to talk about. It's all *anyone* talks about lately.

Even Ernst Resch and his friends are talking about Hitler. They say that Hitler has written a book about his life and it's going to replace the Bible someday.

I didn't think Ernst Resch could read a book that didn't have pictures.

I decided to find out for myself, but when I asked Mr. Heller if he had the book Hitler wrote about his life, you would have thought I had asked him if he had any dead bodies buried in the basement.

Mr. Heller asked if The Doctor knew about it, which had never happened before, so I asked him if I needed to have all my reading requests approved by my father.

He looked a little embarrassed — which was precisely my intention — and said that this was a special case and I would have to ask my father.

I wanted to talk to Daddy alone but the only time was after dinner when he was playing billiards. I know he doesn't like to be disturbed when he's playing billiards because it's one of the few times he *really, really* relaxes, but I just couldn't wait.

He didn't look quite as horrified as Mr. Heller did. In fact, in an odd way, he didn't look surprised at all, like he had been expecting the questions for some time.

He asked me if anything had happened at school and I told him no, it was just that some of the kids are saying that Hitler's going to do this and Hitler's going to do that and not one of them seems to know what they are talking about so I want to see for myself, which, I pointed out, was something he had taught me.

SUNDAY, JANUARY 30, 1938

I always have breakfast alone with Daddy on Sunday morning because Mother likes to sleep late and Max goes to his Zionist meeting. Daddy even lets me make his egg for him so we don't need Milli.

I *love* to watch Daddy eat his breakfast — it's really quite fascinating. I serve it to him in his eggcup and then he takes a teaspoon, carefully cracks the egg all the way around the middle halfway between the equator and north pole, and then (when he's sure he's got it cracked *just right*) he winks at me and topples it, saying "Off with their heads" because that's what I used to say when I was little.

After breakfast Daddy goes for his Sunday walk around the Ring. Daddy believes fresh air and brisk walks are important to your health. He's a fast walker — when we went hiking last summer in the Vienna Woods I had a tough time keeping up with him. He walks the whole four kilometers with his hands jammed into his coat pockets and bent forward as if he were walking into a gale.

MONDAY, JANUARY 31, 1938

I had my midyear conference with Mrs. Thompson today. This is the second year I've had her for homeroom, which is fortunate. Mrs. Thompson is *very, very* sweet, but things didn't go at all as I had expected. She said I seem to have adopted a "very nonchalant" attitude this year, which made me wonder why people never say "chalant," they only say "nonchalant." No one ever says, "You seem very chalant today."

Mrs. Thompson said I was her best student last year but I'm not working as hard now. I seem to be daydreaming quite a lot and if there is anything that is bothering me she would be happy to talk to me about it in the strictest confidence. (But there really isn't so we just sat there looking at each other for a while.) Mrs. Thompson is one of the few people I know who doesn't look like an animal but she does remind me of a willow tree.

She said I am a gifted girl and that I should make sure I don't squander that gift and right then and there I decided to make *squander* my word of the week. Every Monday I choose a word of the week and then I try to use it as much as I can, although not so much that anyone notices. (The only one who pays enough attention to get suspicious is Sophy).

Last week's word was disappointing — not *disappointing* the word, just disappointing. The word was *jeopardy* but I think *squander* will work out much better.

Mrs. Thompson had her red class book open right

on the desk and I tried to read my grades upside down but I couldn't, quite.

THURSDAY, FEBRUARY 3, 1938

When I gave Mr. Heller Daddy's note he took forever to read it, which I don't understand because the note was very short, shook his head for an equally long time, and said he would have *Mein Kampf* by the end of the week.

SUNDAY, FEBRUARY 6, 1938

Dinner last night with Uncle Daniel was even more unpleasant than usual.

First he became utterly furious just because the salt rolls weren't fresh although he slathers so much butter on them I don't know why it would matter. He kept calling for the waiter, who either didn't hear him or didn't want to, for which I couldn't blame him, so Uncle Daniel just threw the whole basket of rolls onto the floor, which was quite embarrassing, although we're all used to it by now.

When the waiter failed to bring the horseradish sauce at the same exact time he brought the boiled beef I was afraid Uncle Daniel was going to throw that on the floor, too. (Although Uncle Daniel was quite perturbed about the "ineptitude" — Uncle Daniel likes to use long words to describe *everything* — of the waiter, he did recover in time to order his cheese strudel with cream sauce for dessert.)

Uncle Daniel is *very* particular about his food. He considers eating — especially when *he's* eating — a sacred act. The only thing that can distract Uncle Daniel from his food is the sound of his own voice.

Uncle Daniel can talk for hours and not be the slightest bit aware that he is so UNBELIEVABLY BORING. He just assumes everything he says is interesting — he leaves no stone unturned and no thought unuttered.

Now he's decided he wants to be hypnotized, which, Max whispered, is a good idea because maybe the hypnotist won't be able to bring him out of the trance.

Uncle Daniel thinks he's a great writer, and I have to admit he is famous in Vienna, although I really don't know why. Everything he writes is grim and gruesome and he doesn't finish anything, anyway, because lately he's been suffering from writer's block. (Well, at least we know he isn't suffering from eater's block or talker's block.)

The worst part was after dinner: Uncle Daniel invited himself back so he could read his latest "work in progress."

This "work in progress" was even more horrible than the last one. Uncle Daniel said this time he's going to write a full-length novel, but we'll see because he usually has more success sticking to his very short stories. The novel is based on the real-life eighteen-year-old daughter of some archduke who lived about a thousand years ago — Uncle Daniel is forever going on about Austrian history and Emperor Franz Josef, his beautiful wife, Elisabeth, and their son Rudolf and his tragic suicide.

The girl's father is so mean he doesn't let her do *anything* or go *anywhere*, which is what most of the story is about (typical of the boring nature of Uncle Daniel's stories). But then one day she's smoking a cigarette (which, of course, she has been forbidden to do) and her father turns up unexpectedly. So she hides the cigarette behind her back, igniting her royal garments, and she is burned to death right before his eyes.

Max laughed himself silly over that one. Mother said it gave her a migraine, and I left to finish my homework.

Later, when I went into the kitchen because I was thirsty, I could hear Uncle Daniel and Daddy talking in Daddy's study. They were having another argument about Hitler.

Uncle Daniel had a lot of wine at dinner, which he always does, and it makes him talk louder than usual, which is pretty loud anyway, so I could hear every single word he was saying.

He said all this worrying about Hitler is unnecessary because once he achieves power he will moderate his extreme views. And besides, Uncle Daniel added, Hitler has done wonders for the Germans — restoring order and a sense of pride among the people.

Then Daddy said something, but Daddy speaks so softly I couldn't hear, even though I had moved down the hall and was standing right outside the door of the study.

Uncle Daniel wasn't listening to a word Daddy was saying, you could just tell. He went right on: Hitler is only after the Polish Jews — he has nothing against the Viennese Jews and besides, Hitler is right. Vienna is being "drowned in Jews as surely as the Danube is over-flowing its banks." They are a miserable, filthy lot. They have no money, no possibilities — they're nothing but "a bunch of Yiddish-speaking shtetl Jews" and they should go someplace else.

Every time Uncle Daniel was silent I knew Daddy was saying something, but I didn't dare come any closer. All I could hear was Daddy saying something about no place to hide and Uncle Daniel shouting, "I am not a Jew. I haven't been a Jew for twenty years. Why should I worry about that now?"

Uncle Daniel *isn't* Jewish, at least not anymore. He was born Jewish, just like us, but he decided to become a Lutheran. Max says he was even baptized.

He's embarrassed that we're Jewish. I remember him once telling Daddy he shouldn't use his hands so much when he talks and Mother that she shouldn't wear her hair up because it makes them look Jewish.

Daddy has a particular way of talking when he's very serious and he was very serious now. I could hear every word.

Daddy told Uncle Daniel he is indulging in wishful thinking if he thinks Hitler is just saying all those awful things about the Jews until he achieves power. And he is a bigger fool if he thinks the Nazis will make a distinction between Polish Jews and Viennese Jews or converted Jews and unconverted Jews. He urged Uncle Daniel to wake up and face facts.

The conversation was scaring me even worse than Uncle Daniel's terrible story did, and I didn't want to hear any more — I just want Hitler to go away and leave us alone. I went back to my room and tried to read myself to sleep, but I couldn't.

Why is Uncle Daniel ashamed that he was Jewish?

Should I be ashamed, too? Did I do something to be ashamed of? If I did, what is it?

MONDAY, FEBRUARY 7, 1938

I remember the first time I knew we were Jewish. I was four and Max was ten and he came home from school with his shirt bloodied and his pants ripped and muddied. Milli shooed me into my room and told me to stay there.

No one said anything that night, and Max didn't come out for dinner, which had never, ever happened before.

The next afternoon I overheard Mother talking on

the telephone to Mrs. Hirsch. She was telling her that a gang of hoodlums had followed Max home yelling vile things at him about being Jewish. Finally Max had had enough and went after the biggest one (which is just like Max) but there were too many of them. They kicked him and stomped him until he was left lying on the ground, unable to move.

From then on I knew I was different but I didn't know why.

TUESDAY, FEBRUARY 8, 1938

We had a substitute teacher today so the boys were even ruder than usual. I think it would be better for all concerned if boys were kept in cages — really, I truly do.

The poor, pathetic substitute was bewildered, which only encouraged Ernst Resch and his sidekick Thomas the Turtle (that's not his real name, I just call him that because he's so slow in the head) to act even more foolishly. The two of them started throwing wet sponges at some of the smaller boys, and by the time order was restored half the class was laughing themselves silly and the other half was crying.

WEDNESDAY, FEBRUARY 9, 1938

Sophy's angry at me again, this time because she got a B minus on her mathematics test and I got an A without, according to her, studying for a minute, which isn't entirely true. (Even if I didn't have to study that much, why is that a reason to be mad at me?) Besides, I asked her, what's the matter with a B minus, which made her even madder. Sometimes Sophy is *so* frustrating. She has to excel at *everything*.

I stayed up very, very late last night reading. I kept promising myself one more chapter, just one more chapter, but as soon as I finished that one chapter I just couldn't bear to go to sleep without finding out what was going to happen in the next one and, although I did sleep a little, before I knew it it was seven and Milli was banging on my door warning me that I was going to be late for school (which I wasn't, but only because I ran for the streetcar and ate my breakfast roll on the way).

We got our report cards today and I did much better than I thought I would. I think Mrs. Thompson was just trying to scare me.

I was hoping to show Daddy at dinner but he wasn't there. This is the second night this week he has had to make house calls late into the evening.

THURSDAY, FEBRUARY 10, 1938

Daddy came into my room late last night and sat on the bed and whispered that there was something he wanted us to talk about, "just the two of us."

He wants me to take English lessons. I told him I am already learning to speak English in school but he said that is not enough. I don't understand. Enough for what?

He's arranged for me to see a Miss Sachs every day after school. He's already spoken to Mrs. Konig and she will no longer be expecting me.

I was speechless. I didn't think Daddy even knew who my piano teacher is let alone where she lives or where to call her.

There were so many questions I wanted to ask, but one look told me Daddy just wanted me to trust him and so I did.

Miss Sachs lives only a few blocks from school, and I am to be certain no one knows I am going there. "No one, Jewel," he said sternly. "Promise," I said. I want Daddy to know he can count on me.

FRIDAY, FEBRUARY 11, 1938

Milli and the new cook (I still don't know her name) have been busy all week getting everything ready for Mother's dinner party.

Mother instructed Milli to use our very best china and be sure the silver is polished to a mirror finish.

There's a crisis *every* hour and the latest one involved the ashtrays. Each of the gentlemen must have his very own ashtray and there seems to be a whole box of them missing.

SUNDAY, FEBRUARY 13, 1938

I must admit Mother did look radiant last night. She wore the blue velvet floor-length gown (the one that took Mrs. Svoboda so long to fit her for that day we went shopping) and a simple strand of pearls. The hairdresser spent nearly all afternoon getting her hair *just right*, but it was a triumph in the end and the rhinestone-studded tortoiseshell combs sparkled and glittered in the candlelight all night long.

Mother's the *perfect* hostess. She has something personal and flattering to say to each guest as they arrive ("You're looking younger every day"; "Where did you get that dress?"; "Why don't we see more of each other?"), kissing them on the cheek, calling everyone "dear," whirling around like a top spinning from room to room, making sure the shy ones are talking to the bold ones, convincing those who are sitting to stand and those who are standing to sit and pouncing the moment she sees any sign of discomfort, discontent, or (heaven forbid) boredom.

She was even pleased with the food, which is a first (so I think the cook can stay on). Milli and the servants she hired for the occasion were twirling around the apartment almost as fast as Mother, making sure everyone had enough caviar, chateaubriand, roast chicken, red cabbage, mashed potatoes, apricot-filled dumplings, cake, and chocolate soufflé.

I didn't eat as much at dinner because by the time we sat down I had already stuffed myself silly with the chocolate-covered coffee beans that were placed in bowls all around the apartment (even in the WC!).

I noticed that Mother decided to play one of her tricks on Uncle Daniel. Uncle Daniel has trouble hearing out of his left ear, although he never admits it, so Mother sat Mrs. Blumenthal on his left because she's the most talkative person in Austria (besides Uncle Daniel himself, of course).

Mother usually suffers Uncle Daniel in silence but not always. One night, last year, she told him he was a profound speaker but a superficial thinker and Uncle Daniel stormed out of the restaurant.

Mrs. Blumenthal was looking her usual gaudy self thanks to her ruby-red dress, far too lavishly applied makeup, huge rings on every finger, and her habit of smoking one cigarette after another so that her head is always partially enclosed within a cloud of smoke. She looks like a giant parrot.

I must admit Mrs. Blumenthal did tell a wonderful joke that completely mortified Uncle Daniel because he likes to let everyone know that he's not Jewish anymore.

Mrs. Blumenthal asked if anyone had heard of the Jewish man who converted to Protestantism and then, right after that, converted yet again to Catholicism.

When the man was asked why he converted twice

he said, That way, if anyone becomes suspicious that he was once a Jew and asks, What was your religion before you were a Catholic? he could say he was a Protestant.

The whole table had a good laugh except for Uncle Daniel, who either was embarrassed or possibly just couldn't hear and was getting angry.

Watching Mrs. Blumenthal and Uncle Daniel was the highlight of the dinner, and I could tell by the amused look on Mother's face that she was thoroughly enjoying the fruits of her labor.

Mother was in such good spirits that she even told the story of when she and Daddy had to elope because her family did not approve of their marriage on account of Daddy's family not being rich like Mother's. (I think that's why we never see any of them.)

After dinner Mr. Heller proposed a toast "to our lovely hostess, the most beautiful woman in all of Vienna." Of course he doesn't know that every year Mother tries her best not to invite him because he's just a shopkeeper, but Mr. Heller is the one person who Daddy insists on inviting.

The topic of conversation over cognac and cigars (Milli had found the ashtrays just *hours* before) was the same as it's been for weeks now: Hitler, what is happening in Germany, and what is going to happen in Vienna.

The discussion was even more spirited than usual because of the surprise announcement on Radio Vienna this afternoon that Chancellor Schuschnigg is meeting Adolf Hitler in Berchtesgarten.

Almost everyone agreed that the Chancellor will most certainly set matters straight now that he is finally meeting Hitler face-to-face. Mr. Blumenthal added that Hitler's crazy ideas might be all right for the Germans but he won't get very far with them here in Vienna.

Daddy and Mr. Heller were strangely quiet and kept looking at one another as if there was some secret they shared.

I wish I knew what Daddy and Mr. Heller were thinking but I'm afraid to ask. I don't think they are as optimistic as the others. I'm not, either.

Max went right to his room after dinner, and I wanted to talk to him so much that I decided to risk knocking on his door.

He was rolling one of his cigarettes (actually he's gotten quite good at it) and, at first, he looked annoyed that I had disturbed him. But when I told him why I'd come he softened and was like he used to be.

He said he wasn't going to lie to me. They are all underestimating the seriousness of the situation: ostriches sticking their heads in the sand and hoping Hitler will just go away. But, Max said, Hitler isn't going to go away.

He offered me a puff of his cigarette and I took it because I didn't want him to think I was afraid.

For what seemed like the longest time, we sat there in silence, broken only by the sound of the dinner party going on outside.

Finally Max spoke. He said only when the Jews are in Palestine will they be safe and not until then.

But I can't believe that. I won't believe that. Why should we not be safe here? We are living in Vienna.

MONDAY, FEBRUARY 14, 1938

Miss Sachs's apartment building doesn't even have an elevator and, since her apartment is way up on the top floor, I had to walk up nine flights of regular stairs and then, as if that wasn't enough, climb up this winding iron staircase that goes nearly to the roof. Her tiny apartment is the only one on the whole entire floor — you would hardly know it is even up there.

She's not nearly as old as I thought she would be and she certainly teaches English differently than they do in school. For one thing, she speaks perfect English — she doesn't even have an accent — but she talks so fast I can barely keep up. When I complain she laughs and warns me that soon we will be speaking only English (I honestly don't see how that is possible).

The best part is the last half of each lesson. We listen to gramophone records by American singers. Miss Sachs says this will improve my pronunciation and make it more authentic.

Today we listened to the Boswell Sisters and they are *terrific*. My favorite song is "Between the Devil and the Deep Blue Sea." Next week we're going to listen to someone named Ella Fitzgerald. She's a Negro.

Miss Sachs says that by the time we're done I will speak English just as well as she does, but I think she's saying that just to be nice.

Even though Miss Sachs lives in the opposite direction from Mrs. Konig I still turn right when I leave school as if I was going to my piano lesson. Then I walk all the way around the block because if Sophy sees me going a different way she will wonder why and start asking all sorts of questions I don't have answers for. I've never really lied to Sophy about anything and I don't want to start now.

Daddy said to be certain *no one* sees me. Although I'm not sure why he's so insistent about this (now that I think about it, I don't even understand why it's so important that I take English lessons), Daddy must have a good reason. Especially because Mother thinks I'm still taking piano lessons! I asked Daddy what would happen if Mother ran into Mrs. Konig and he said I should take care of learning English and he would take care of Mother and Mrs. Konig.

Ernst Resch was watching me today, standing there surrounded by his friends. At first I was worried that, somehow, he knew where I was going, but I think he was just being his creepy self.

TUESDAY, FEBRUARY 15, 1938

Sophy told me at recess that Mr. Erickson started talking about the Jews right in the middle of the geography lesson. He had this big map of the world up in front of the class and was pointing to one country after another asking anyone if they could name each country and tell him what they all have in common.

Mr. Erickson said that what they all have in common is that the Jews who live there are considered a plague and not wanted because they are inferior in every way to the Aryan race, which is a superior race and destined to rule the world.

Sophy wanted to say something but was too afraid.

She said it is *awful* being in Mr. Erickson's class and that I am lucky to be in Mrs. Thompson's.

SATURDAY, FEBRUARY 19, 1938

I finally agreed to accompany Uncle Daniel to his favorite coffeehouse. He's been asking for *weeks and weeks* and my feeble excuses were getting pretty obvious and, besides, he usually behaves himself better when it's just the two of us. I must admit I do enjoy seeing all the strange and interesting people who congregate there, but of course the *real* reason I decided to go was that Daddy asked me to: "Your uncle likes to show everyone how beautiful his niece is," so how could I say no?

Uncle Daniel practically *lives* at the coffeehouse. He gets his meals there, takes his phone calls, and his friends stop by and leave messages. The only thing he does at his apartment is sleep and I'm not even sure about that.

The coffeehouse is always filled with men who look like they have nothing better to do than sit around talking and drinking *café au lait*.

Every time I come I see this one man who sits by himself, scribbling away furiously in his notebook and glowering at anyone who comes even remotely near his table.

If he doesn't want to be bothered, why doesn't he just write at home? I suppose it's because he feels lonely there. If it were me, I would write at home.

He wears a black patch over one eye. It was supposedly injured in a fencing duel with a rival writer who insulted him in print.

A small glass of green liquid is always in front of him. Once he was so absorbed in his writing that he put his cigarette out in the glass — I was hoping he would drink it but at the last minute he noticed.

I asked Uncle Daniel what it was and he said, "Absinthe," and ordered me a glass before I could stop him.

It didn't taste nearly as good as it looked — quite the opposite, as a matter of fact. It wasn't cool and refreshing — it was bitter, burned my throat, and tasted like licorice of all things.

Uncle Daniel and his writer friends have their own table right under the skylight next to where the chess players gather.

I like to watch them play, even though I only understand which way the pieces move and not much more.

Daddy and Max play every Tuesday night, but they're too incredibly boring to watch. Sometimes I think it's not really a chess game but a contest to see who can take the longest time *considering* where to move without actually moving.

The chess players at the coffeehouse move much faster, and each time they make a move they smack down their buttons on top of this double clock device that sits between them.

When I was smaller I would just turn around in my seat and peek, but one day a man winked at me and motioned for me to come over. I swiveled around that instant and pretended that I hadn't seen him. But a couple of minutes later, when I thought for sure the coast would be clear, he was still watching me and again motioned me over, patting the seat next to him. I'm usually pretty shy with strangers, but he looked like a nice man so I went over.

He said I was welcome to watch them play any time I wished and he called me "young lady," which made me blush, although I don't think he noticed.

When someone makes a move that the onlookers think is either really brilliant or really stupid they oooh and aaah or shake their heads in disbelief. It's really very funny.

The chess players are a lot more fun than Uncle Daniel and his friends. All *they* ever talk about is themselves.

If you took the word "I" out of their vocabulary, they wouldn't be able to communicate at all. They talk about the most insignificant things and no one really listens to what anyone's saying.

Hugo-von-something-or-other is the worst. He's a poet. He wears a top hat and checkered trousers, has no chin whatsoever, reeks of tobacco, and talks in this really, really high voice while waving his hands around like he's pretending to be a schoolgirl.

According to Uncle Daniel he paints his toenails.

SUNDAY, FEBRUARY 20, 1938

At one o'clock today, Radio Vienna broadcast Hitler's speech from Berlin. It was the first time they've ever broadcast one of his speeches. He has an Austrian accent, which shouldn't surprise me since he was born here.

There must have been a lot of people because you could hear them all shouting *SIEG HEIL SIEG HEIL*, when he arrived.

His voice was hoarse — probably from all that ranting and raving he usually does. Although he sounded crude, there is something about the way he speaks that makes you listen. It was like when I'm on the Ferris wheel at the Prater and I look down even though I know I shouldn't because I'll be scared.

He went on and on: The speech lasted for three hours.

Daddy was disappointed that Hitler didn't say anything about his meeting with Chancellor Schuschnigg, but relieved he didn't say anything awful about the Jews, the way he usually does.

Max said it was obvious the meeting didn't go well.

(There have been reports that Hitler shouted at the Chancellor and humiliated him.)

Uncle Daniel listened with us and he assured everyone that it would all blow over. That what is happening in Germany is not our concern.

Daddy said Uncle Daniel talks like Hitler is on the other side of the world, rather than just three hours away.

MONDAY, FEBRUARY 21, 1938

Ernst Resch said hello to me this morning, which was odd, because he has never said hello to me before.

All day long it bothered me. There was something not quite right but I couldn't put my finger on it. Then, tonight, while I was brushing my teeth, it came to me.

He didn't say, "Hello, Julie." He said, "Hello, Jew Lee," just like that, Jew Lee, separating each syllable and grinning like the Cheshire Cat.

I'm not going to tell anyone about it, though. It would just make things worse.

TUESDAY, FEBRUARY 22, 1938

We listened to Ella Fitzgerald today. I have never, ever heard anything like that. She is *the best* and my favorite song is "Someone to Watch Over Me."

Next week we're going to listen to Helen Ward, but I just want to keep listening to Ella Fitzgerald.

Miss Sachs said there are more people each day who want to learn English in case they have to emigrate.

I never thought about that. We could never leave Vienna. Daddy's office is here and we have always lived in Vienna and, besides, where would we go? But then, why is Daddy having me take English lessons?

WEDNESDAY, FEBRUARY 23, 1938

Mother is very upset. Mrs. von Schaukel, "The Beauty Queen of Vienna," canceled her facial for the second week in a row.

Everyone is looking forward to Chancellor Schuschnigg's speech tomorrow.

THURSDAY, FEBRUARY 24, 1938

Daddy said he thought the Chancellor's speech sounded hopeful, but Daddy sounded more hopeless than hopeful.

Too little, too late, Max said.

FRIDAY, FEBRUARY 25, 1938

Daddy gets upset every time he reads the newspaper now. I asked why he just doesn't stop and he said he wants to know what is going on.

MONDAY, FEBRUARY 28, 1938

Daddy asked me how my lessons with Miss Sachs are going and I told him fine. He asked if anyone has seen me coming or going. I've never seen Daddy so concerned.

I asked Miss Sachs if she gets tired of teaching English all day — I just assumed that's what she did — but in the mornings she teaches retarded children.

She gave me a good-bye kiss. She doesn't wear

any makeup or lipstick so I don't have to worry about wiping it off so no one will ask me who kissed me.

Now we sing "Someone to Watch Over Me" at the end of *every* lesson! Miss Sachs puts her arms around my shoulders and we sing really, really loud — but not as good as Ella.

"Someone to Watch Over Me"

There's a somebody I'm longing to see
I hope that he
Turns out to be
Someone who'll watch over me.

I'm a little lamb who's lost in the woods
I know I could
Always be good
To one who'll watch over me.

TUESDAY, MARCH 1, 1938

Milli is working on Hitler's horoscope. She said he is an Aries, which, according to her calculations, is ruled by Mars, which means he's courageous, impulsive, willful, and certain to accomplish great things.

I found a small picture of Hitler in the drawer of her night table. I'm sure I'm the only one who knows about it but I don't want to say anything.

I'm afraid to ask her about it because she might ask what I was doing looking in her drawer. (Actually, I was looking for a deck of playing cards, but she would *never* believe that.) I'm also afraid of what her answer might be. She's changed since Hitler's speech. She's not the same Milli I knew.

WEDNESDAY, MARCH 9, 1938

There is to be a vote this Sunday to see whether or not we will remain an independent country or be joined with Germany. Everyone hopes the vote will end all of this frightful worry about the fate of our country.

THURSDAY, MARCH 10, 1938

People are running all over Vienna painting pro-Austrian slogans on the sidewalks and buildings; there are marches and demonstrations in every district; vans drive around; while planes drop leaflets urging all to vote YES for Austrian independence and YES to remain free of German rule. Everyone is going to vote for Chancellor Schuschnigg and not for Hitler. It is all very exciting.

FRIDAY, MARCH II, 1938

There is *not* going to be a vote!

There was a special announcement on the radio and then they just returned to the music like it was just another day in Vienna.

All the color is drained out of Daddy's face, although I can see that he is trying to conceal his concern from me.

More *horrible* news! Chancellor Schuschnigg has *resigned*. German troops are about to invade our country.

He doesn't want bloodshed so he has ordered the army not to fight.

He is giving up — letting the Nazis take over our country without firing a shot!

SATURDAY, MARCH 12, 1938

Hitler is coming to Vienna!

Everywhere they are preparing to welcome him.

Swastika flags are flying from the buildings and there is even a gigantic banner with his face hanging on the Kärtnerstrasse.

SUNDAY, MARCH 13, 1938

German bombers are flying low in formation overhead; wave after wave of them fill the sky and the sound of their huge engines makes the ground tremble.

Max said he heard rumors that German troops have crossed the border and are headed our way.

He thinks there will be war, but he always thinks the worst.

TUESDAY, MARCH 15, 1938

Hitler is here!

In Vienna!

He spoke from the balcony of the Hofburg.

Schools, shops, and factories were all closed so that everyone could come out to greet our new leader. Hundreds of thousands of jubilant Viennese filled the streets and formed a torchlight procession through the inner city as church bells chimed incessantly in celebration of our union with Germany.

We are no longer Viennese. We are no longer Austrians.

We are all Germans now, just like that.

We have no country.

WEDNESDAY, MARCH 16, 1938

I am frightened even to write. My hand trembles as I do.

Late last night Mr. Heller called to warn us that they were attacking anyone in the street who even looked Jewish. People were being pulled from taxicabs and streetcars and beaten.

While Daddy was talking to Mr. Heller there were shouts coming from the street. I started toward the window but Max pulled me away.

He turned off the light and slithered along the wall and pulled back the curtain. There were trucks filled with men and there were swastika flags flying from the trucks as they drove. He still couldn't make out what they were shouting.

Then the trucks were passing right below us. So

close I could feel the building shaking, and now I *could* hear what they were saying. They were screaming: *KILL THE JEWS, KILL THE JEWS, KILL THE JEWS.*

All of a sudden there was someone banging so hard on our door that the walls were shaking worse than the building. No one moved and no one spoke. Milli came out of her room to see what all the banging was about and right before she got to the door it burst off its hinges, came crashing to the floor, and all these horrible men streamed into our apartment.

Some of the men went right over to our piano and began pushing it toward the balcony window. Then they pushed it up and over the railing and it landed on the streets below with a horrible crash.

Everything was happening at once.

They dragged Daddy and Max out into the hall and down the stairs. Then they started toward Milli who screamed, "I'm just the maid, I'm just the maid. I'm not Jewish like them. I'm just like you, Heil Hitler, Heil Hitler," and she pointed to Mother who was sitting next to me on the couch, trembling. "She's the one you want. She's the rich Jewish bitch." Milli's face contorted, her mouth twisted into a senseless grin, and her eyes gleamed as if she were possessed.

Obeying Milli's command, the men turned around and looked at Mother.

One of them pulled her off the couch so violently I thought her arm would come off, but the other said, "Wait."

I recognized him when he first came in but he averted his eyes when he realized who I was and where he was. He was the policeman Daddy had taken care of! The one who broke his arm and cut his eye. His cast was off and his eye had healed but it was him. I remember because Daddy wouldn't even let him pay and the man said he didn't know how he would ever thank him, and now here he was, dragging my mother into the streets.

For a moment I thought he was going to let us go, but the other one told Mother to put on her "fine Jewish jewelry" and her "fine Jewish furs." He kept calling her "rich Jewish bitch" over and over and grinning just like Milli.

I jumped up, hoping to go with Mother. I didn't want to be left alone, but the other man pushed me back onto the couch and said if I was smart I would stay put.

Mother came out wearing her blue velvet gown,

diamond necklace, emerald earrings, and ermine cape. They dragged her, too, out into the hall and down the stairs.

I was all alone, except for Milli, but I didn't even know if she was still in the apartment.

There was shouting from the hall and the sound of heavy boots going up and down the stairs.

I didn't know what to do. I just sat there, too scared to move or call out.

I must have fallen asleep although I tried my hardest not to, because the next thing I knew I heard voices. Familiar voices.

It was Daddy, Mother, and Max.

They looked filthy and frightened and Mother's blue velvet gown was badly torn and her jewelry and furs were gone. But there was no blood. No one was hurt. They were all alive.

I gave each of them a big hug. I had never hugged Mother before. I never realized how small she is. She isn't any taller than me and she looked different. Something *was* different. It was like I was seeing her for the first time. Like a mask had fallen from her face revealing someone I didn't know very well.

Daddy spoke, although he looked as if each word

was costing him dearly. He said everyone should go to bed.

I hoped Max would come to my room and explain everything the way he did when I was younger. Fortunately, after only a few minutes, there was a soft knock and he entered holding an ashtray in one hand and a lit cigarette in the other.

Outside they were given buckets of water and toothbrushes and told to clean off the pro-Austrian slogans from the sidewalks. They did as they were told, but after a while they realized that it wasn't really water, it was some kind of paint stripper, and their hands began to blister.

The acid burned their fingers and hands, but every time they stopped one of the men kicked them and told them to continue while people stood around watching, laughing, and shouting "WORK FOR THE JEWS, WORK FOR THE JEWS, AT LAST THE FÜHRER HAS MADE WORK FOR THE JEWS!"

Then they were told to form two straight lines and spit in each other's face. One man refused and they immediately poured gasoline all over him and lit a match. The man tried to give in, he screamed that he would do it, but it was too late.

I thought they were all together because they were all together when I saw them, but Max says that he and Daddy were taken down the street as soon as they got outside and never even *saw* Mother. She was sitting in the downstairs foyer when they got back and didn't say a word then about what happened and hasn't since.

I wonder if the Duchess is right when she tells Alice that everything's got a moral, if only you can find it.

FRIDAY, MARCH 18, 1938

Richard came back from Mrs. Svoboda's with Mother's blue velvet gown untouched. Mrs. Svoboda said it would be better if Mother took her dresses elsewhere because she no longer serves Jews.

MONDAY, MARCH 21, 1938

Someone wrote GET OUT JEWS in big, big letters all over the blackboard in Sophy's class, and Mr. Erickson didn't even erase it when he came in — he just taught the class and left it up there for all to see.

TUESDAY, MARCH 22, 1938

Ernst Resch and his friends are wearing Hitler Youth badges on their shirts now.

Mrs. Thompson is keeping a sharp eye on them but she hasn't as yet said anything.

I wish Sophy was in my class, then I wouldn't feel all alone.

WEDNESDAY, MARCH 23, 1938

Daddy has had the front door lock repaired. He's put in a double lock, even though we all know that won't do us any good.

Mr. Pisk no longer comes — Daddy shaves himself in the morning and makes his own breakfast and I get ready for school the same as usual, only Milli's gone.

Nobody knows where she went — all we know is that she's gone. I went into her room for the first time since that night and the only things left were mine. Just my toys, dolls, and books remained on the nearly bare bookcases. It was like she was never here.

FRIDAY, MARCH 25, 1938

Each day we hear stories, one more horrible than the next.

Mr. Heller's store was broken into and the cash register smashed with a hammer. There are Jewish stars painted all over the windows, and Mrs. Heller has to stand outside every morning with a sign hanging from her neck saying DO NOT BUY FROM US. WE ARE JEWS. She says only Jewish customers come in now, and she doesn't know how long they can go on like this.

Mr. Friedman told Max that people come in with their children and allow them to take any candy they want now, and they tell them that they don't have to pay because the store is owned by Jews.

They came to Mr. Blumenthal's apartment the same night they came to ours and as soon as they knocked he just opened the window, shouted a warning to anyone standing below to get out of the way, and jumped eight floors to his death, leaving Mrs. Blumenthal to care for herself and their three children.

The worst is the little Eckstein boy, Jakob. When they came to take his father away, Jakob ran to him and held onto his leg. Mr. Eckstein tried to shake him off but little Jakob just held on tighter, screaming, "Daddy, don't go, Daddy, don't go." Then one of the Nazis grabbed him by the hair and threw him backward so that he hit his head on the corner of the bed so hard that he died that very instant.

It's all right to do anything you want to someone if they're Jewish.

Everything has changed.

People who were friendly neighbors and shopkeepers only yesterday now proudly wear swastikas on their lapels and, when they pass you on the street, either make a mean comment (but not loud enough so that you can hear what they are saying) or just look the other way as they walk on by.

People are such cowards, really. At heart, people are cowards.

Now they think they're better than we are simply because they are not Jewish. What a world — just *not* being Jewish is enough to make you feel superior.

I never thought about being Jewish before all this started. I mean, I knew I was Jewish but that was all. What makes us Jewish? Am I Jewish just because Hitler says I am? When I walk down the street, people don't look at me because I have blond hair and green eyes. They don't think I'm Jewish, they think I'm Aryan.

We don't go to synagogue, not even on the really important holidays — and even Sophy's parents go then.

"Three-day Jews," Daddy calls them, because for three days a year they are religious and then, after that, nothing.

Max is the only one who acts like he's Jewish and that's just because he's a Zionist.

Daddy says it doesn't matter if there's a God or not. He says that too many people spend too much time worrying about what they're going to do when they get to heaven and too little time considering what they're doing right here on earth.

I asked Sophy if she believes in God and she said she does. I asked her what she imagines God is like and she said she thinks He is a very, very old man who lives way up in the sky watching what is going on all over the world and keeping an eye on everyone.

I'm not sure about any of this. I'm not sure there's someone watching over everyone. How could there be someone watching over everyone? Christians? Jews? Nazis? Viennese? Germans? *Everyone*? Is the same God who's watching over me the same one who watches over Hitler?

Sophy prays every night that God will come down from heaven and save us. I wish I could pray for that, too, but I just can't. If He can do something about all the terrible things that are happening, why doesn't He?

Maybe there's a God and maybe there isn't. Maybe everything happens by accident, like two balls colliding in midair — who can say for certain what will occur after they make contact? Maybe people just like to think there's a God because it makes them feel better.

I'd like to feel better, too, but not if it means fooling myself.

I spent all day pretending I was Alice and no one could tell.

"'For it might end, you know,' said Alice to herself, 'in my going out altogether, like a candle. I wonder what I should be like then?' And she tried to fancy what the flame of a candle looks like after the candle is blown out. . . . "

MONDAY, MARCH 28, 1938

This morning, as I was leaving for school and waiting for the elevator, I heard Hermann Danzer's mother saying good-bye to him and reminding him to "Stay away from the Weiss girl — don't talk to her. It's too dangerous."

Now I am so dangerous — like I carry some kind of disease — merely talking to me could kill you.

Maybe, I thought, I could run up to Hermann at recess, yelling at the top of my lungs, "Hermann, Hermann," and then fling my arms around him and say how brave it is that his family has invited mine for dinner even though we are Jewish, and then watch him squirm.

Maybe I would go all over Vienna. Go around purposely scaring people by pretending to recognize them and talking to them and touching them like they were old friends and watching them flee in horror.

TUESDAY, MARCH 29, 1938

Sophy and I went to the cinema. I didn't want to go but Sophy made me. I like to go to the cinema so I can forget everything that's happening now, but it was a bad idea. We sat near Katty and Pauline, who are in Sophy's class, and as soon as we sat down they got up and moved to the other side of the theater.

I told Sophy that's the last time I'm going.

Fortunately, the Nazis haven't been able to stop me from reading yet.

I went into Daddy's library to find a book and decided to read *Main Street* by Sinclair Lewis. I like the title and besides, I know it's one of Daddy's favorite books, not only because it was in the glass bookcase but also because I've heard him and Mr. Heller talking about it. Daddy says that Sinclair Lewis is a great American writer.

WEDNESDAY, MARCH 30, 1938

Uncle Daniel is gone!

Just disappeared in the night and nobody knows for sure where he has been taken.

Daddy has not heard from him in some time and was worried. When he came back he was white and drawn. He said Uncle Daniel's clothes were all there and that someone had broken into the apartment.

Daddy insists that everyone follow the usual routine as best they can. Life must go on, he says.

THURSDAY, MARCH 31, 1938

Mrs. Thompson gave the entire class a stern lecture today. She wanted to remind everyone that what is apparently acceptable in the streets of Vienna — "strutting about and carrying on" — is most certainly not going to be tolerated in the classroom.

School, she said, is a sacred place. We can't study other civilizations properly if we are acting in an uncivilized manner ourselves.

I held my breath the whole time she spoke. Finally, someone had enough nerve to say something. I was so proud of her.

FRIDAY, APRIL 1, 1938

Mrs. Thompson is gone! Mr. Erickson was sitting in her place when I arrived this morning, and he announced that she would no longer be teaching at the school. He gave no explanation for this extraordinary event.

He said we are going to be combined with his class, and just as he was saying that Sophy's class filed in, but before they could find seats, Mr. Erickson announced that all Jews should step to the back of the room and wait.

Then some older boys marched in carrying pails of soapy water and proceeded to wash some of the chairs including the one I had been sitting on.

Mr. Erickson said he didn't want any Aryan children sitting in seats made dirty by Jewish children.

He looks like a crow — a big, black crow. He has greasy, slicked-back hair and black eyes, and he's always looking around suspiciously.

MONDAY, APRIL 4, 1938

On the way home from school yesterday, some boys jumped out of nowhere, grabbed me, and put an awful-smelling handkerchief under my nose.

It made my eyes tear badly and made me feel faint. I fought the feeling as hard as I could, but I fell to the ground anyway.

One of them leaned over me and said that if I told anyone, I would pay dearly, and then they ran away.

I know whose voice it was. It was Tommy the Turtle and I think one of the other boys was Ernst Resch, although I couldn't be sure because he had a cloth around his face. But Ernst is so tall (he's the tallest boy in the grade) that I'm almost sure it was him.

I don't know what to do. I'm not going to tell anyone, not Daddy because he has too much to worry about or Max because he would get too angry.

Today in school I did not look at Ernst Resch or Tommy the Turtle and they didn't look at me. I think they're afraid I might tell, so I'm lucky because then they might leave me alone.

TUESDAY, APRIL 5, 1938

Daddy tries to act like everything will be all right, but I can tell that he's just pretending and underneath he's concerned.

He and Mother are still distraught because of what happened last week. Mrs. Hirsch gave birth to a healthy baby boy and then, the next morning, she awoke at dawn, wrapped him carefully in a blanket so he wouldn't get cold, held him tight in her arms, and jumped out of the hospital window, killing them both.

She left a note behind that said she could not let her son live in a world gone mad.

She's right — our country has been taken over by madmen.

I wish, like Alice, we could all change size, go through the keyhole, come out the other side, and be on Main Street.

THURSDAY, APRIL 7, 1938

I slept late again this morning. There's nothing much to get up for now that there's no school for Jewish kids. The longer I sleep, the less time I have to be afraid.

I was awakened because someone was talking in the hall, right outside my door.

It was Mother and Richard. I opened the door just a crack, but I could see them both — Richard was standing just inside the doorway, holding his chauffeur's cap in his hands.

Mother was being nicer to Richard than I had ever seen her be. She was patiently explaining to him that since we are no longer permitted by the authorities to have a car, we don't need a chauffeur.

Richard just stood there not saying anything — like

he didn't understand — so Mother said that meant we didn't have any work for him and that she would do her best to help him find another job and then the two of them just stood there silently facing each other.

When Richard started to speak, I could hardly hear a word he was saying. He always talks with his head down like he is embarrassed and now he was mumbling even worse than ever.

He said he thinks what is happening is wrong and that he doesn't know why it is happening. He said he could still accompany Mother on her shopping trips and help carry the packages just like always.

They could even use his little Fiat. Although it isn't as fine as our car, it is in good running condition.

There were tears welling in Mother's eyes. She thanked Richard and told him she would discuss the situation with Dr. Weiss.

Mother seems to be getting worse with each passing day. She stays in her room with the curtains drawn all the time — especially since Mrs. Hirsch.

She looks like a ghost — pale and thin — and she walks around in a daze. I have never seen her like this. Her eyes are open but she doesn't see. She speaks but only when spoken to. It's like her body is here but there's nothing really inside.

No one really knows for sure what happened that night to Mother.

FRIDAY, APRIL 8, 1938

Daddy came home late again last night. He didn't even come in to give me my good-night kiss.

One of Max's friends was jumped by four thugs who grappled him down to the ground, pinned his arms to the side, and put a cigarette out in his hand. Then they told him if he cried out they would slit his throat.

Max has stopped going to the university.

"'If everyone minded their own business,' said the Duchess . . . 'the world would go round a good deal faster than it does.'"

MONDAY, APRIL 11, 1938

All I do all day long now is read. There's really nothing else to do.

We are not allowed to go to the cinema, the museum, the library, the woods, or the park — there is a sign that says: DOGS AND JEWS FORBIDDEN. We can't even play in our own courtyard. Max meets his friends in the Jewish cemetery because it's one of the few places you can go.

I don't even go for my English lessons anymore. Miss Sachs isn't there.

Every day there are new rules to follow if you're Jewish: Don't use the elevators; don't sit on park benches; don't go into public places.

Daddy said it is a good time to catch up on my reading. Daddy always tries to make the best of everything.

I've taken all the books I want to read from Daddy's library and organized them in the order in which I will read them.

TUESDAY, APRIL 12, 1938

I don't even get undressed anymore when I go to sleep at night — I just get into bed, read until I get sleepy (which takes a very, very long time), pull the covers tight all around me (I'm always cold), and then cry as quietly as possible so no one will hear me.

I *never* feel rested — in the morning I'm just as tired as I was the night before.

When I wake, my hands are clenched so tight they hurt. Each night I dream the *same exact dream*. I dream that I wake up one morning and this never happened. There is no Hitler. No men broke into our apartment and shattered our lives; Mrs. Thompson is still my homeroom teacher; Mother didn't look the way she does — none of it has happened and everything is just like it was. But then I realize that *the dream* is a dream. *This* is real and I have to get up, get out of bed, and face another horrible day.

It's really quite curious, as Alice might say.

One day you're worried whether you should cut your hair short or leave it long, part it in the middle or off to the side, use a barrette or no barrette.

And then, the next day, you're worried that your family is going to be rounded up by the Nazis and taken who knows where.

Now the thought of doing anything at all with my hair makes me laugh out loud. I wear the same thing day after day, and caring what I look like is a distant memory.

The first thought I have in the morning and my last thought when I shut my eyes at night is, How long can this go on?

"'I can't explain *myself*, I'm afraid, sir,' said Alice, 'because I'm not myself, you see.'"

WEDNESDAY, APRIL 13, 1938

Last night the doorbell rang, and I was certain I would be taken away. I promised Daddy I wouldn't answer if he wasn't home but I couldn't stop myself. "Who is it?" I whispered, and it was Mr. Graf, the butcher.

He was having trouble speaking and had a bottle in one hand and a big gun in the other.

He had come to stay the night to protect us from "Hitler's hooligans." He said that The Doctor has always been a good man, taking care of people when they are sick even if they don't have the money, and he was going to make sure that nothing happened to him.

I had quite a time convincing him that I would be all right and that he should go home.

FRIDAY, APRIL 15, 1938

Mother is dead.

She killed herself.

I long to go to sleep but I am afraid to shut my eyes for fear I will see her coffin.

I held Daddy's hand the whole time but I didn't cry. I was the only one. Daddy cried. Max cried. Mr. and Mrs. Heller cried. But not me. I didn't want to cry.

The sun was shining and the sky was a brilliant blue — just the kind of day Mother liked best.

The kind of day we would all go to the Prater. Mother liked to go to the Prater — it was the only time I saw her laugh. She went on all the rides: the merry-go-round, the giant Ferris wheel — she even went on the roller coaster.

The only place she wouldn't go was the sideshow because she didn't like to see the calf with two heads or the lady with no stomach.

Sometimes we would have ices, eat outdoors in one of the gazebos, and even stay up late for the fireworks.

When it was sunny Mother would come alive, like a flower unfolding.

She hated the rain. "What a gray day," she would re-peat throughout the day, as if somehow, if she said it often enough, it wouldn't be true.

Max found her.

He called Daddy at his office and told him to come quickly.

I went into her room. It was cold and dark.

She was lying quietly on the bed.

Her pillboxes and little glass vials were all empty.

I whispered, "Mother," but she didn't move. She looked like she was sleeping very, very soundly.

I heard Daddy calling people and telling them that she died of pneumonia. No one was surprised. No one asked any questions. No one said, "I didn't know she was so sick. Was it sudden? Wasn't there anything you could do?"

When he got off the telephone, he must have known what I was thinking.

"It's better this way, Precious Jewel. The truth will serve no purpose." That's what he said.

(The truth will serve no purpose. Maybe I *have* become Alice.)

My hand is shaking badly — I can hardly write. It doesn't feel like pen on paper but knife on stone.

I wish I could be like Sophy. I wish I could believe that there really is someone up there, and if you pray long enough and hard enough he will listen to you.

Even though I didn't believe there is anyone, I offered up a prayer. Please, God, I said, take my mother as a sacrifice. Be satisfied; let her life be enough. Spare us any further suffering. Let us live.

I listened in absolute silence for the longest time, hoping I could feel His presence so that I would know that my prayer had been heard. But I could feel nothing, and the only sound was my own breathing.

WEDNESDAY, APRIL 20, 1938

Daddy was taken to the police station today. He was picked up while he was making some house calls. They made him stand there for hours with no food, water, or explanation, and then he was thrown into a van and taken to a huge army barracks and put in with hundreds of other poor souls.

They were made to run in between SS men who kicked them and struck them with their rifle butts. Daddy was lucky — others were taken somewhere else for interrogation.

MONDAY, APRIL 25, 1938

Daddy looks so tired and sad. His green eyes used to sparkle like he was just about to let you in on a big secret, but now they are dull and lusterless.

Three of his patients died from heart attacks this past week because of the hideous things they were forced to endure.

The Nazis patrol the streets constantly, and you can be picked up without warning and taken away at any time.

There is no use trying to hide. They have the names and addresses of all the Jews in Vienna. There are rumors that any day now they are going to go from house to house and send us far, far away.

Max has heard about camps just for Jews. His friend's father returned from one of these camps but won't say anything about it because he doesn't want to be sent back.

People are starved there and some are killed as soon as they arrive.

This is the first time I have heard about any camps.

Max heard about a lady who boarded a train carrying a small suitcase, which she took with her into the

WC. After a few minutes, she came out in a long, white wedding gown, calmly walked down the aisle smiling at everyone, and when she got to the end, walked in between the cars and threw herself off the speeding train.

FRIDAY, APRIL 29, 1938

Daddy still goes to the office every day, despite the risk.

He has lost some of his Gentile patients, although not all, because many of them know that Daddy is the best.

It is very dangerous for him to go to work, but there is no talking sense to him. He says his patients need him. Max goes out every night and that, too, is dangerous. Daddy doesn't approve, and they argue, but Max ends up going anyway.

I have an easier time of it because I am blond. To be blond now is good. If you're blond, you may walk in the streets without fearing for your life. If you're blond, you don't have to worry about what's around every corner. If you're blond, you can look someone in the eye and not be afraid of what you'll see.

Although I do have to go get food at shops that are far from our apartment so they won't know me, won't know that I am Julie Weiss — Jew.

This morning a couple stopped their car and asked me if I wanted a ride. They both had gold swastika pins on their lapels.

I was going to run, but they were looking at me so adoringly that I realized they didn't see the real me at all. All they could see were my Aryan looks and therefore I was safe. I was invisible. Their foolishness made me bold and I got into the back seat.

On the way they told me that they have always wanted to have a girl, but they hadn't been blessed with one yet. If they were, they hoped she would look just like me.

I told them they were embarrassing me and I actually blushed.

When we got to the store, I thanked them for the ride and they said, "Heil Hitler" and so did I.

On my way back from the grocer's I saw a group of SS soldiers in their hideous black-and-silver uniforms pushing around a blind boy. They were in a circle pushing him from one to the other while tears of terror streamed down his poor little face.

I didn't dare look for long and just scurried on my way.

The world I knew is collapsing all around me, and I can only stand by and look on in helpless horror and mute disbelief. There is nothing I can do.

SUNDAY, MAY 1, 1938

Daddy asked Max and me to sit down because he had something very important to talk to us about.

He said that Mother had written to Aunt Clara and Uncle Martin just before — that's all he said — "just before"— and we understood.

I didn't even know anyone knew where Aunt Clara and Uncle Martin lived in America. Daddy said that he and Mother had their address in New York City, and that if we are to leave Vienna we will need an affidavit from someone in America — someone who will vouch for us and assure the authorities that we will not become a burden to the American government.

If we don't get an affidavit, we can't get a visa, and if we can't get a visa, we can't get out of Vienna.

Daddy said we can't stay here — it isn't safe. The Nazis want all the Jewish people out of Vienna.

That's why Mother wrote to them. I couldn't believe Mother actually wrote to her sister. We were always forbidden to even speak her name.

This is the first I have heard about any of this. About leaving. I don't want to leave Vienna. This is my home.

Daddy said Aunt Clara is a year younger than Mother, almost as pretty, and has been an actress since she was a little girl. There used to be all these *huge* scrapbooks around the house with Aunt Clara's press clippings. Uncle Martin was a coin dealer when he lived in Vienna and in America he is a financier on Wall Street.

I wonder if Wall Street is near Main Street?

Max only wants to go to Palestine. He says Jews are not wanted anywhere, and what's happening now won't stop until there's a place for Jewish people to go. There must be a Jewish state if we are to survive.

Daddy thinks Max's ideas are foolish and dangerous and that's why they argue.

I don't know what to think. Max's beliefs are so strong and certain — at times I wish I could be like him. But I'm more like Daddy.

Some people are getting divorced just so the wife can get a job as a housemaid in England (they only want unmarried women), then they can send for their husbands later.

People are desperate to find relatives in America who can send them the precious affidavits. Affidavit has become a magic word — it means life. Daddy says one of his patients has a copy of the New York City phone book so he can see if he has any relatives living there who can sponsor him.

TUESDAY, MAY 3, 1938

Max took Mother's jewelry, her fur coats, and the gold watch Daddy gave him for his birthday to the pawnshop and came back with some money so I was able to get some food for dinner. He says we have used up all our savings. I don't know what I would do if it wasn't for him.

I am learning to mend our clothes as we haven't any money to spare for new ones and even if we did, no one would sell any to us because we are Jewish. I made myself a very colorful scarf from a torn blouse that didn't fit anyway and turned one of Max's old jackets into a vest. I made him try it on — which he didn't want to do in the *worst way* — and then I made him admit that it looked quite nice.

I couldn't stop myself from giving him a hug and, much to my surprise, he hugged me back. A great, big hug, which, for the moment, made me feel safe and warm.

At least we're better off than Sophy's family. They burned down her father's clothing store two weeks ago and now they have no money for food.

Her mother stands in line for hours each morning at the soup kitchen.

Yesterday Sophy said her mother came home with nothing. The Nazis drove up in their trucks, pushed over the tables, spilling the soup all over the floor, and then drove away laughing.

MONDAY, MAY 9, 1938

A synagogue in Leopoldstadt was burned to the ground today. It was filled with worshipers when someone threw a burning torch into the building — it's a miracle only a few people were injured and no one was killed.

THURSDAY, MAY 12, 1938

Fear is everywhere.

It's in the air I breathe. The water I drink. The food I eat. It's on the tip of everyone's tongue and can be seen in every eye.

MONDAY, MAY 16, 1938

Sophy is going to England!

Her parents are putting her up for adoption! That is the only way they can get her out of the country. They have no money and no affidavit.

It was dangerous for her to come to tell me, but she was afraid that we wouldn't have a chance to say good-bye. She looks terrible. Her eyes are red from crying and she also doesn't sleep because she is too afraid. She has lost weight and appears to be weak and listless, which is so unlike Sophy.

I am happy for her. Happy that she is going away from here, even though I will miss her terribly.

I wouldn't want to go, though. I wouldn't want to be separated from my family even if it meant I would be safe.

TUESDAY, MAY 17, 1938

Daddy spent another day waiting in line at the American Consulate near the Ring. It was just another disappointing day.

He's gone by the time I get up because the lines start forming at dawn and go all the way around the block.

He says there are people there who applied for visas years ago.

There are so many documents you have to get: transit visas, certificates of conduct, tax forms, and then each one has to be signed and stamped properly.

Sometimes it takes so long to get one of the documents that by the time you get it one of the others has expired, and you have to start all over.

And sometimes you can wait in line all day and when you finally see someone you are told you have filled out the form wrong or are waiting in the wrong line, and you have to begin the process all over again.

FRIDAY, MAY 20, 1938

Each day we hope for the affidavit from Aunt Clara and Uncle Martin. It has been weeks and weeks and we have heard nothing. Daddy says we can't even be sure they got Mother's letter. He isn't certain they are still at the same address or even if they're still living in New York City. They might have moved and then we are waiting for nothing.

TUESDAY, MAY 24, 1938

Mr. Heller bought boat tickets from some people who said they were document experts, but they turned out to be phony and now the Hellers are stuck. They have no money, no tickets, and Mr. Heller's store is closed since there are no longer any books. On Sunday, a mob broke into the store, threw all the books into the street, and burned them in a huge bonfire.

WEDNESDAY, MAY 25, 1938

Even though Daddy has lost more patients recently, the ones who remain seem to be getting so sick as to make up for it.

FRIDAY, MAY 27, 1938

I've gotten used to being hungry. At first I thought I wouldn't be able to stand it — that gnawing, empty feeling. But now I've gotten used to it, so it isn't too bad.

SUNDAY, MAY 29, 1938

Daddy was up late again with papers spread all over the dining room table. I kept him company.

He said he heard a good joke while waiting in line today. An official told someone who was applying for a visa to come back in the year 2001, and the man who was applying asked if he should come back in the morning or the afternoon.

I don't know how Daddy can laugh.

MONDAY, MAY 30, 1938

Sophy has left.

All at once I realize how much she meant to me. While she was here, in Vienna, I believed I could endure all that was happening, as horrible as it might be. *We* would be all right, somehow. Just knowing that she, too, was suffering a similar fate made it almost bearable.

Now that she is gone I suddenly feel uncertain and alone.

TUESDAY, MAY 31, 1938

Max has left, too.

When I awoke a piece of paper had been slipped under the door. On it Max had written, in his neat, tiny handwriting, his favorite Rilke poem:

> God speaks to each of us as he makes us,
> then walks with us silently out of the night.
>
> These are the words we dimly hear:
>
> You, sent out beyond your recall,
> Go to the limits of your longing.
> Embody me.
>
> Flare up like flame
> and make big shadows I can move in.

Let everything happen to you: beauty and terror.
Just keep going. No feeling is final.
Don't let yourself lose me.

Nearby is the country they call life.
You will know it by its seriousness.

Give me your hand.

There was also a note on the dining room table but it hardly said anything. All it said was that he was going where he belonged. By that he means Palestine. I think Max didn't say more because he was afraid of who might read it.

Daddy was sitting there reading the note when I came in, tears streaming down his gentle face.

How I wish I didn't have to see Daddy cry.

FRIDAY, JUNE 3, 1938

Daddy said some men were coming to see him tonight, and no matter what happened, I shouldn't come out of my room.

When I heard them come in, I lay flat on the floor,

hoping I could hear what they were talking about under the door. I could hear patches of conversation here and there, but most of it was drowned out by the sound of shuffling feet as people came in and out of our apartment.

Then there were more voices, louder than the first ones. They were laughing and having a good time, going up and down the elevator and carrying things. This went on for nearly an hour, and then finally it was quiet and Daddy knocked on the door and said it was all right to come out.

I didn't know what I expected to find when I came out. These days it could be anything. Thankfully, Daddy looked all right so I was relieved.

Then I saw the walls. And the floors.

They were bare. All our pretty paintings and beautiful rugs were gone. All of them, gone. The only thing left on the walls were the nails the paintings had hung on. The men had taken everything.

I didn't want to cry. I wanted to say something, but so many thoughts were crowding my mind that nothing — not one of them — was able to make its way out of my mouth.

They're only paintings, Precious Jewel, Daddy said, only paintings.

FRIDAY, JUNE 10, 1938

The letter from Aunt Clara and Uncle Martin arrived today. Aunt Clara writes that she will vouch for us and they will meet us when we arrive in New York City. All we have to do is let her know when that is.

I jumped into Daddy's arms and gave him the biggest hug, but he didn't hug me back. I could feel him shrinking from me.

He said that our lives have been shattered. That I must be brave and pick up the broken pieces and go on.

Why was he saying this to me?

What was he hiding?

Then he told me.

He isn't going. He isn't going to America. He wants me to go without him. He has known this all along.

He could never leave. His sick patients need his help. They depend on him. He can't just abandon them. He wouldn't be able to live with himself if he did.

He needs to know that I am far, far away from here, safe in America.

I told him I want to be with him. That I can stay and help with his patients. That he wouldn't have to worry about me.

But I had to stop because of the tears that now finally came, bursting forth from a place so deep inside me I was unable to reach in and stop them.

Looking at Daddy I knew that all my words wouldn't be enough to change what is happening to us, and that the only thing I can do for him is to say as little as possible.

"'Would you tell me, please, which way I ought to walk from here?'

'That depends a good deal on where you want to get to,' said the Cat.

'I don't much care where —' said Alice.

'Then it doesn't matter which way you walk,' said the Cat.

'— so long as I get *somewhere*,' Alice added as an explanation.

'Oh, you're sure to do that,' said the Cat, 'if you only walk long enough.'"

SATURDAY, JUNE 11, 1938

It was dark and still in my room last night and I was thankful for that. I lay there with my eyes wide open, staring into the blankness, seeing nothing.

I wondered what it would be like to be dead. Would you know? Would it hurt? Was it like sleeping or "going out altogether, like a candle"?

I wondered what it was like when I was first born, unable to talk or reach out and touch whoever was holding me.

Slowly the sun filled my room with morning light, and I wondered what it would be like in America.

PART TWO

NEW YORK, NEW YORK
1938

MONDAY, JULY 11, 1938

Last night I had the dream again.

I am sleeping in my bed, the one back home, in Vienna. There is someone else in the room. I can feel it. When I open my eyes, Daddy and Mother are standing at the foot of the bed, like they've been waiting there for me to wake up.

Mother is wearing her blue velvet evening gown — the one she wore that night. She even has on the same sapphire earrings, and her gown is torn at the shoulder, just as it was then.

She looks happy — like she is going to a ball and doesn't realize what has happened to her.

Daddy looks sad — like he *does* know. He seems far away, even though he is standing right next to Mother. He is about to say something, I am sure of it. But his face remains motionless, frozen.

Mother puts her hands on Daddy's shoulder, to comfort him. Then Mother starts to speak, but although her lips are moving, she makes no sound.

"Louder, Mother," I say, but she doesn't hear me and just keeps moving her lips, filling the room with silence.

"Louder, Mother," I keep repeating.

Daddy is holding his hands over his ears, and I am afraid the sound of my voice is hurting him.

The next thing I know, Aunt Clara is holding me and I am soaked with sweat. She holds me in her arms and hums a tune that sounds familiar, and I fall asleep.

Aunt Clara comes in each night to look in on me. I pretend I'm sleeping because I don't want her to worry. It does make me feel better, though. It reminds me of when Daddy would come in and give me my good-night kiss.

WEDNESDAY, JULY 13, 1938

I have been sleeping for days. I wake up and wonder where I am but I am so tired, I just fall back to sleep.

The journey across the ocean seemed to take forever. I was so sad. I didn't talk to anyone, even though people tried to be nice to me. All I could think about was Daddy and Max.

When we finally arrived, a morning mist darkened

the sky. Occasionally the incredibly tall buildings emerged from the fog, their needle-point tops piercing the sky.

New York City looked more like a fairy-tale castle than a real city.

I was in America and I was afraid.

Afraid someone would stop me from leaving the ship and make me go back to Vienna. Afraid no one would be there to meet me. What would I do then?

The pictures Daddy gave me only showed Aunt Clara when she was young, but I recognized her immediately. She looked so much like Mother.

I worried that she wouldn't like me. That they regretted doing this and only did it because they had to. Because they felt sorry for me.

They took me back here and said I should get some rest. I hoped there would be a letter from Daddy when I arrived but there wasn't.

I remember someone bringing me toast in the morning, and soup later in the day. I ate some of the soup but mostly I just left it on the night table.

FRIDAY, JULY 15, 1938

I wrote Daddy a letter.

Today is his birthday. Max's, too. This is the first time I have not been with them.

I told Daddy that I arrived safely and how nicely Aunt Clara and Uncle Martin are treating me. I know that will make him happy. I asked him if he could write as soon as possible.

Aunt Clara promised me she would mail it without delay.

SUNDAY, JULY 17, 1938

I've had a headache and fever for the past two days. I always get a headache after I have that dream.

Susie said I should put the hot water bottle behind my neck. She's the one who brought me the soup. I did, but it just doesn't help.

Aunt Clara wants the doctor to see me. I've assured her I will be fine. I don't want to see a doctor.

MONDAY, JULY 18, 1938

I did something I shouldn't have. I just couldn't stop myself.

I went into one of the other bedrooms when no one was around. Aunt Clara and Uncle Martin must be very, very rich. Our whole apartment in Vienna could fit into their living room. I counted the number of rooms — there are *sixteen.*

I was looking for something to wear.

All I have are the clothes I took in that little suitcase Daddy gave me. Everything is filthy and smells awful from the boat.

It was Eva's room.

I didn't even know Aunt Clara had a daughter. I don't even know if Daddy or Mother knew.

She must be a very good tennis player, because there are lots of photographs of her playing tennis and holding trophies. She looks much older than me, maybe seventeen or eighteen.

I don't know where she is or when she's coming back.

Eva is a very organized girl. She keeps all her socks neatly rolled into balls and lined up according to color.

In one of the drawers I found some packets of

letters tied with string. They were addressed to: MR. AND MRS. MARTIN SINGER and were from EVA SINGER, THE WAUWINETT INN, NANTUCKET, MASSACHUSETTS.

The envelopes had already been opened, so it was just too tempting.

The letters were written last year, and even though they were kept in order, I still didn't understand everything.

Eva apologized for not writing sooner and said she wasn't angry anymore. She talked about her "condition" and someone named Dr. Webb, so I know her "condition" is a medical one.

She says she tires easily and naps during the day. She is sure she is doing the right thing, although she doesn't always sound so sure. She's glad that Susie is there with her.

She says it's just as beautiful as ever, and each morning she walks along the ocean and in the evening watches the sun go down on the harbor side.

Included in one letter was a list of clothes she wanted Aunt Clara to send her. And in another letter she says that there are days when she feels lonely.

TUESDAY, JULY 19, 1938

Today I wore a violet dress I found in Eva's room, but Susie told me it would be best if I put it back in "Miss Singer's" closet.

Susie didn't say anything, but it was obvious I had done something wrong.

WEDNESDAY, JULY 20, 1938

Aunt Clara gave me some iron pills. She said that Dr. Webb thinks they will help build up my strength. I wonder if it's the same Dr. Webb mentioned in Eva's letters. It must be.

THURSDAY, JULY 21, 1938

Aunt Clara bought me the most wonderful clothes: skirts, blouses, dresses, and shoes — and they all fit perfectly. Everything's lightweight because she says New York is very hot in the summertime — even hotter than Vienna.

I should have gone to the shop with her, but I just

don't feel like going out yet. Maybe soon. Maybe tomorrow or the day after that.

SUNDAY, JULY 24, 1938

My room is very pretty. It's recently been painted pale blue. (I can still smell the paint.) There's a desk (where I'm writing now) that has a top that rolls down, and all these little drawers and compartments to put things in. My bed has a beautiful white canopy over it.

Mrs. Parrish made me lunch. She's the cook.

WEDNESDAY, JULY 27, 1938

Aunt Clara is a famous actress. I found all these large scrapbooks that are filled with hundreds of articles, reviews, and pictures of her. They were in the room with the piano and all the plants.

The scrapbooks go back to when Aunt Clara lived in Vienna, when she was six and known as "Baby Clara."

The American newspapers call her "a delicate beauty" and "one of the reigning geniuses of the American theater."

The biggest articles are about when she played Juliet

in *Romeo and Juliet,* and Nora in *A Doll's House,* although I don't know what that is.

She's played in theaters all over America: Chicago, Boston, Atlantic City, New Haven, Washington, and Los Angeles.

She's in a play now, *Peter Pan.* Rehearsals begin next week. She's Mrs. Darling, Wendy's mother.

THURSDAY, JULY 28, 1938

There isn't a single, solitary moment that I'm not wondering where Daddy and Max are and what they're doing.

I *try* not to think about it because it's hard for me to breathe and I get frightened.

Sometimes I try so hard *not* to think about them that the inside of my head feels twisted into a giant knot.

MONDAY, AUGUST 1, 1938

Uncle Martin works on Wall Street. That's where Max says all the money in America is kept. I'm not sure what Uncle Martin does on Wall Street.

He leaves every morning at eight-thirty.

Even though they have a chauffeur, Uncle Martin prefers taking the subway to work every day. He says it's faster and much more fun.

Uncle Martin has sad eyes — he looks like a baby seal.

I went downstairs with him this morning. I sat outside on the fountain.

It was Susie's idea. She said that I didn't have to go out if I didn't want to, but that didn't mean I had to stay "cooped up" in the apartment all day.

I didn't know exactly what "cooped up" meant, and Susie explained it to me. "Coop" is what they call the cages where they keep chickens, and since it's pretty cramped they call it "cooped up."

Susie introduced me to "Red Mike" and "Black Mike." They're the doormen. Susie calls them "Red Mike" and "Black Mike" because one has red hair and the other has black skin, just like her.

She's the only one who calls them that, though. She said I should call them by their regular names: Mr. Nicolson ("Red Mike") and Mr. Smalls ("Black Mike"), which is pretty funny because Mr. Smalls isn't small at all.

Susie said if I needed her she would be right upstairs "tending to my business." I've started a list of some of the things she says, like "cooped up" and "tending to my business," so I can talk like an American.

I'm wearing the clothes that Aunt Clara bought me, so I don't look like a foreigner.

The building is quite big — it takes up the whole, entire block. And it's very, very luxurious. Beautiful glass lamps and colorful rugs and paintings are in the lobby.

Right outside there is a big stone archway with a black iron gate you drive through when you come in from the street. Then there's a drive-around courtyard, where the chauffeurs and taxicabs come, and a fountain right in the middle — that's where I sit.

I just watch "Red Mike" and "Black Mike" blow their shiny, silver whistles so people can get taxicabs; show the delivery boys where the service entrances are; take in packages; and hold the doors for everyone.

With their white gloves, gold-braided caps, and long uniforms, they look like they're guarding the queen's palace.

WEDNESDAY, AUGUST 3, 1938

Aunt Clara asked me to help her prepare for her new role as Mrs. Darling in *Peter Pan.* I read the lines that come before hers, so she could practice. Rehearsals begin Friday.

THURSDAY, AUGUST 4, 1938

Even though the two Mikes are very kind to me, my favorite is Mr. Esposito.

He always greets me the same way every day: "Hiya, Toots. What's a beautiful girl like you doing on a beautiful day like today?" He only says, "Hiya, Toots" if I'm alone, though. If I'm with Uncle Martin or Aunt Clara, he just says, "Good morning, ma'am."

He lets me operate the lever that makes the elevator go up and down, and is going to let me help him polish the wood and clean the mirrors.

I told Mr. Esposito about my decision to add "Hiya, Toots" to my list of American words, and he said he was happy to be of help.

FRIDAY, AUGUST 5, 1938

Aunt Clara went to rehearsal today. She was concerned that I would be all right. I assured her I would be. Besides, Susie is here with me.

I spent most of the day, though, with Mr. Esposito. He tells me about all the people who live in the building.

There's Mrs. Lowenstein in 3B, who smokes her cigarettes from a long cigarette holder. She has three dogs: Niña, Pinta, and Santa Maria, and every morning she takes them for a walk in Central Park (which is right across the street). The dogs are so fat, their stomachs rub the ground. Mr. Esposito said that Uncle Martin once told Mrs. Lowenstein that she should put roller skates under each dog.

Mr. Esposito calls her "The Mad Hatter" because of all the wild hats she wears. I must say that every time I've seen her, she has had on the most extravagant hat. When she gets on the elevator, Mr. Esposito says, "My, what a lovely hat you're wearing today, Mrs. Lowenstein," and then he turns to me and winks.

According to him, she has the largest collection of antique clocks in the whole world. He says she spends all day running around her apartment making sure they're working properly.

This morning Mr. Esposito stopped the elevator on the third floor, and we tiptoed down the hall to 3B. Just as we got to the door we could hear all the clocks striking eleven.

Mrs. Lowenstein is so fat that one of the Mikes has to get her a special taxicab with a back seat she can fit into.

Mr. and Mrs. Cassidy live in separate apartments on different floors, even though they're married. Every morning they meet in the lobby and go out for breakfast together, which I think is very romantic but Mr. Esposito thinks is "fishy."

Then there's Mr. Allen. He's a writer. He wears two pair of glasses, although not at the same time. When one is on his face, the other hangs around his neck by a string. He looks real funny and spends all day in a bathrobe that's so badly torn at the elbows, you can see clear through to his pajamas. He never, ever steps outside the building, because he is very concerned about "microbes." He has all his food and groceries delivered.

Mr. Allen doesn't smile because of his teeth. A number of them are missing, but he won't go to the dentist. He doesn't like to be touched by anyone.

He wears shoes without socks and has recently had

his apartment soundproofed because all the noise in New York jangles his nerves.

Sometimes he has a wild look in his eyes, as if he's in great distress.

I saw a girl my age in the lobby one morning, but she looked away when she noticed me.

SATURDAY, AUGUST 6, 1938

Aunt Clara says that what Mrs. Lowenstein needs is another husband. The first one died the first year of their marriage when he fell asleep smoking in bed and set their house on fire. Fortunately Mrs. Lowenstein was out at the time.

Uncle Martin said she'll never get a husband because she wears too much cheap perfume. But Aunt Clara said she saw Mr. Lippman "giving her the eye" the other day. Mr. Lippman's the one with the hearing aid. His sister lives in Berlin, and he is hoping she will be able to go to England before it is too late.

Each year Mrs. Lowenstein throws herself a lavish birthday party, and the invitations say NO

MONOGRAMMED ARTICLES because she returns everything for cash no matter what it is.

Uncle Martin says she has two reserved seats at Carnegie Hall. One for herself and one for her coat, so she doesn't have to sit next to anyone. *And* her gloves have to be custom-made so that the fingers are big enough for her huge diamond rings to fit.

Once Aunt Clara had a heart-to-heart with her and tried to convince her to see a psychiatrist (Uncle Martin calls them "brain gazers"), but Mrs. Lowenstein said she has hundreds of friends who will listen to her problems for free so why should she pay someone twenty-five dollars an hour?

SUNDAY, AUGUST 7, 1938

Aunt Clara always looks a little sad to me, with her raccoon eyes. Not an everyday sadness, but like there is some deep sadness lurking just below the surface — far enough down so that you can't quite make out what it is, but near enough that you can see it.

WEDNESDAY, AUGUST 10, 1938

Being in America is not like merely being in another country. It's more like being on the moon.

I am not as frightened as I was, though.

THURSDAY, AUGUST 11, 1938

Susie suggested we go to the Central Park Zoo. It's only a short walk, so I agreed to go.

Besides not liking the smell, I didn't like seeing the animals locked up in those horrible cages.

I know Susie took me there because she thought I would like it, but I had to pretend I was having a good time.

There was the saddest polar bear in this tiny, tiny pool. It wasn't much wider than he was long. He just kept swimming back and forth, back and forth. He kept it up the whole time I was there, and each time we walked by I tried not to look but I just couldn't help it. There he would be, swimming back and forth, back and forth.

I almost started to cry but I didn't. I thought I was doing a good job of pretending, but as soon as we got back to the apartment, Susie said, "I suppose we won't be going back there real soon."

FRIDAY, AUGUST 12, 1938

New York is louder than Vienna. Fire engines and police sirens scream, cars and taxis honk, and the elevated trains rattle noisily all through the day.

Ladies wear lots of makeup and too much jewelry, even if they aren't rich. And not everyone in New York is rich, like Max said they were. I saw one man who earned his money holding umbrellas for people as they came up from the subway.

People in New York chew gum, use toothpicks, spit, and throw their trash in the streets.

SATURDAY, AUGUST 13, 1938

Aunt Clara is unlike Mother in almost every way.

Her face is so expressive — you can always tell what she's thinking. And even though Aunt Clara is very rich, she isn't a show-off about it.

TUESDAY, AUGUST 16, 1938

It's been a month now. I still have not received a letter from Daddy. Every day at five-thirty when Uncle Martin brings the mail up, I run out to see. He always shakes his head sadly, knowing how disappointed I am.

I know Daddy would write if he could. Why can't he?

Uncle Martin said that maybe the mail isn't getting out of Vienna. He has called someone he knows at the American Consulate. He says, "These things take time."

WEDNESDAY, AUGUST 17, 1938

I had the dream again last night. It was the same as the other times, only this time I was *certain* Daddy was going to speak to me, but he didn't.

I try not to think about Daddy during the day. I feel like a dam holding back the ocean: If I let go, I'll be swept away.

I wish I could be happier when I'm around Aunt Clara and Uncle Martin. They have been so nice to me.

But I feel so sad inside, and I'm afraid it shows on the outside.

I don't talk about what happened in Vienna because I don't want to burden them any more than I already have. And, besides, I don't know if they would understand — if *anyone* who wasn't there would understand.

FRIDAY, AUGUST 19, 1938

Each morning we sit in the sunroom, where Aunt Clara has all her plants. She grows the most glorious orchids. It's really a terrace with a glass roof. It's her favorite room, and mine, too. You can look out and see Central Park laid out before you like a gently rolling green carpet.

I read the lines that come before hers and she says hers. It's truly astonishing to hear Aunt Clara speak her lines. She becomes completely transformed. Most of the time she isn't satisfied with the way she does it, and we do it again.

When I read the lines to her she asked me if I had ever taken acting lessons in Vienna or performed in any plays. I told her I spent a lot of time last year pretending to be Alice in Wonderland, which she thought was very funny.

Watching Aunt Clara laugh makes me happy. Her whole face lights up, like she's glad that something can be that funny. Maybe that's why she likes Uncle Martin so much — he always makes her laugh.

She thinks I have a good voice for the theater. That's the first thing you need. "If no one can hear what you're saying, it doesn't matter what you're saying or how you're saying it," she says.

According to Aunt Clara, you can teach someone to sing or to dance, but not to act. You have to be born with it. I have a natural talent. I never thought about it, but I guess I do.

She wants me to read my lines with more feeling so she can respond more realistically.

Tonight I stayed up late reading the script so I could help Aunt Clara.

MONDAY, AUGUST 22, 1938

Susie is taking me to the orthodontist on Wednesday. Aunt Clara said I have to have someone look at my braces.

TUESDAY, AUGUST 23, 1938

I like American food better than Viennese food. Mrs. Parrish makes a delicious meal each night. It's a shame Aunt Clara won't be home for dinner most nights once the play starts.

This week Mrs. Parrish made fried chicken with mashed potatoes; roast beef and gravy; and Lobster Newburg.

Every Friday she makes banana cream pie for dessert because that's Uncle Martin's second favorite. His first favorite is cheesecake, but he says Mrs. Parrish doesn't know how to make "proper" cheesecake, which makes Mrs. Parrish a tiny bit angry, I think. I asked him what "proper" cheesecake was, and he said he would show me.

My favorite is the salad dressing. It's called Thousand Island dressing, and it's so good, I eat it with a spoon. Mrs. Parrish said I eat too much salad and not enough meat, but it's *so* good. No one seems to know, however, why they call it Thousand Island dressing.

They have all sorts of different candies here in America. Black licorice shoestring candy; long white strips of paper covered with colored candy buttons; Life Savers; and Susie's favorite cookie, Mallomars, which I don't really like. She has a whole drawer full of them in her room.

WEDNESDAY, AUGUST 24, 1938

Aunt Clara thinks she needs to lose weight to play Mrs. Darling. I really don't see why. It doesn't say anywhere in the script that Mrs. Darling is skinny. But Aunt Clara is certain that Mrs. Darling is someone who would watch what she eats. So now she has black coffee (she used to put in lots of cream and sugar) and half a grapefruit for breakfast.

She's so willowy and slender, I don't see why she's worried. If it were me, I couldn't eat like that. Even if it was a really, really big part.

FRIDAY, AUGUST 26, 1938

I think "Black Mike" likes Susie. There's just something about the way he tips his hat and says hello. Not only that, but if "Red Mike" is there to keep an eye on things, he insists on carrying her packages all the way to the top floor, where our apartment is. I have never seen him do that for anyone else.

"Black Mike" has Mr. Esposito go right to the sixteenth floor, even if people are buzzing.

He calls it his "express service," and tells Susie there is no charge. Susie laughs and says, "The price is right."

I asked Susie about it when we went down to the basement laundry room to see what was taking the laundress so long with the ironing.

Susie says I have an "overactive imagination" and that Mr. Smalls is nice to everyone, not just her.

I may have an overactive imagination, but I'm not blind, although I didn't say that.

MONDAY, AUGUST 29, 1938

Last night I was thirsty and I went into the kitchen for a drink. Much to my surprise, Aunt Clara and Uncle Martin were sitting at the table, talking. They must have been talking about something they didn't want me to know about, because they stopped and Aunt Clara looked upset.

Uncle Martin was eating a bowl of ice cream and he

handed it to me and asked if I wanted some. Like it was the most natural thing in the world for the three of us to be in the kitchen eating ice cream like there was nothing wrong.

I couldn't help it — I burst into tears, and Aunt Clara put her arm around me, pulled me to her, and said, in the softest whisper, maybe it would be better if I talked about it, and so I did. I told them everything. *Everything,* as the tears streamed down my face so furiously, I didn't even bother to wipe them away.

TUESDAY, AUGUST 30, 1938

Uncle Martin has been begging me to play this silly game he invented called "Sober Sue."

"Sober Sue" was a performer years ago who bet that no one in the audience could make her laugh. If they did, they got one thousand dollars. But no one ever did, even though some famous comedians came down to the theater.

When she retired, one of the newspapers reported that her face was actually paralyzed and she couldn't laugh even if she wanted to.

The game is to see who can make whom laugh first.

I've put Uncle Martin off for days. I think he's trying to cheer me up, and I appreciate it but I just don't feel like being cheered up right now.

I don't want to be rude, however; I owe them so much. So I agreed to play.

Yesterday he told me three jokes in a row: the one about the scarecrow that was so scary, the crows brought back corn they had stolen two years earlier; the one about the inventor of rubber pockets for waiters who wanted to steal soup; and a really boring one about the guy who was so cheap, he put his fingers down a moth's throat just to get the cloth back.

Uncle Martin's jokes aren't very funny, but my funny faces aren't working any better. So far, it's a stalemate.

WEDNESDAY, AUGUST 31, 1938

Mrs. Lowenstein invited me for lunch tomorrow. She said I should come at noon. Mr. Esposito said Mrs. Lowenstein likes "young folks." I wonder if she liked Eva, and if she knows where Eva is.

Every evening when Uncle Martin comes up with

the mail, he shakes his head, meaning there is still no letter from Daddy. Then he puts the mail in the big bowl on the stone table in the hallway and goes into the kitchen to look for something to eat.

My heart starts pounding as soon as Uncle Martin opens the door. I tell myself not to hope, but I can't seem to stop. Just a word or two, that's all I need. Just a word or two.

THURSDAY, SEPTEMBER 1, 1938

Uncle Martin and I were in the elevator yesterday when Mr. Allen got on. Uncle Martin told Mr. Esposito a joke. (Mr. Esposito *loves* Uncle Martin's jokes.)

Mr. Allen had to hold his hand over his mouth because he was about to laugh and expose his toothless grin.

He looks like a turtle when he does that. He draws his head back into his body like a real turtle.

FRIDAY, SEPTEMBER 2, 1938

There must have been more than two hundred clocks in Mrs. Lowenstein's apartment, and just as I walked in they all started to chime twelve. I felt like I was in some kind of fantastic church.

There was so much food, I thought for sure others would be joining us, but no one did.

The dining room table was covered with bowls and platters of shrimp, celery, olives, radishes, creamed potatoes, and two roast chickens, one for each of us.

Mrs. Lowenstein ate hers with her fingers, devouring each piece until there was just a plate of bones lying in front of her.

I tried not to stare, but it was hard not to. She didn't speak at all during lunch because she was concentrating so hard on eating her chicken.

Then she put one of her cigarettes into her long cigarette holder and she asked me if I was going to eat any more of my chicken. When I said no, she snatched it away from me, cut all the meat off the bones, divided it equally onto three plates, and put the plates on the floor for the three dogs, who gobbled it up greedily. Now I know how they stay so nice and plump.

SATURDAY, SEPTEMBER 3, 1938

I went to dinner with Aunt Clara and Uncle Martin for the first time tonight. I just didn't want to say no to them anymore.

Aunt Clara had to go to a cocktail party given by Mr. Garfinkel, who is producing *Peter Pan,* so we were to meet her at the restaurant.

Uncle Martin had Patrick, the chauffeur, pick her up at the party. We walked. Uncle Martin doesn't like to take the limousine that much.

The restaurant was called Tavern on the Green, and it's right in the middle of Central Park. (That's the on-the-green part, I think.) I was greatly relieved that we didn't have to go near the zoo.

It was very fancy — all the ladies wore their furs and diamonds. Uncle Martin said the meal was so expensive, he was thinking of bringing an armored car with gold bullion the next time.

Aunt Clara and Uncle Martin don't drink wine; they drink "martinis straight up, very dry." I asked Uncle Martin what "straight up" meant and he said without ice, and I asked him why he didn't just say without ice and he laughed, although I'm not sure why.

I wanted to ask him what "dry" meant, because they looked pretty wet to me, but decided not to.

He's going to teach me how to mix martinis, which, according to Uncle Martin, is one of the ten most important things you can know in life.

I asked him what the other nine were, and he said he didn't want to tell me because then I wouldn't have any reason to stick around.

He reluctantly agreed to tell me one, which was: Never have a business lunch. Business lunches, Uncle Martin says, will kill you faster than almost anything.

Uncle Martin takes his lunch with him in the morning. Mrs. Parrish makes him a sandwich, which he stuffs into his briefcase along with a banana.

Rehearsals are not going well. Aunt Clara is angry at Mr. Buttinger (who plays Mr. Darling) and at Mr. Robie (who is the director) because they speak French when they don't want her to hear.

What's even worse is that the girl who is playing Wendy keeps fluffing her lines, and Aunt Clara thinks she is too "temperamental." Every time Mr. Robie criticizes her, she starts crying and her mother takes her home. It's disrupting the entire cast, and the play is scheduled to open on October 15.

Aunt Clara saw Mrs. Lowenstein at the Algonquin Hotel, which is Aunt Clara's favorite place to have lunch. She was leaving just as Aunt Clara was coming in and apparently had had a bit too much to drink.

She stumbled into the lobby and miraculously landed safely on the seat in the telephone booth. Then, looking bewildered, she shouted so that everyone in the dining room could hear her, "Where has that damned elevator boy gone to now?"

Uncle Martin said that reminded him of the two brothers who owned a fish market in a small town. One day they had a very bad argument and the younger brother left and opened another fish market right across the street from the original one.

Since the small town could not support two fish markets, both suffered.

The older brother was very, very angry because his younger brother was ruining his business. Each night he prayed on his knees for God to help him. One night, much to his amazement, God actually spoke to him. He would grant him one wish, but there was a condition: Whatever wish he granted would go double for his younger brother. The older brother thought and thought and finally said, "I want to be blind in one eye."

I must admit it was one of Uncle Martin's best stories, and I *almost* laughed but forced myself not to.

After dinner we walked down Fifth Avenue and looked in all the store windows. There are more stores on Fifth Avenue than even on the Kärtnerstrasse, and Fifth Avenue is almost as wide as the Ring.

Aunt Clara and I linked arms as we walked — we're almost the same height.

SUNDAY, SEPTEMBER 4, 1938

Weekdays, Uncle Martin is one person but on the weekends, he's another. That's when he likes to take his photographs. Uncle Martin is more interested in photography than almost anything else. Even more than listening to his favorite comedians on the radio.

During the week his hair is always neatly combed, and he wears a different suit every day. But not on Saturday and Sunday. Then, he wears his white shirt with the torn pocket and frayed collar, and his baggy pants that are stained from the stuff he uses to make his pictures in the darkroom. He doesn't even bother to shave. He looks like someone who was recently shipwrecked on a desert island.

Bright and early he packs his cameras (he never takes just one) in his equipment bag with all the pockets, and he doesn't return until dark.

"Light," Uncle Martin says, "waits for no man."

TUESDAY, SEPTEMBER 6, 1938

I took a walk by myself today and found a second-hand bookstore that reminded me of Mr. Heller's.

There was a man smoking a pipe and reading a book at the front counter. He asked me if I wanted any assistance, but I didn't say anything, as memories of Vienna overwhelmed me. I just shook my head no, turned, and walked out.

It looked like a nice bookstore. The kind Mr. Heller would have liked.

WEDNESDAY, SEPTEMBER 7, 1938

It's very frustrating playing "Sober Sue" with Uncle Martin. He has a great deal of self-control, so even when I make a very good face and he's about to laugh, he just doesn't.

I have two more words for my list that I got from Uncle Martin: "swell," which doesn't mean to get large, and "baloney," which has something to do with lying.

THURSDAY, SEPTEMBER 8, 1938

This morning Uncle Martin gave me, Aunt Clara, and Susie presents, even though it's *his* birthday. He believes that on your birthday *you* should give everyone you love a gift rather than the other way around.

He gave Susie a box of Mallomars, Aunt Clara a silver necklace in a blue box that said TIFFANY & CO. on it, and a yo-yo and roller skates for me.

Uncle Martin can make the yo-yo do all sorts of tricks. Each one has a name: rock the cradle; over the falls; around the world; walk the dog.

But I was most interested in trying out my roller skates. It was a cold but sunny day, and "Red Mike" helped me put them on.

At first I fell more than I skated, but after a while I got pretty good at it and skated all the way around the block without falling once.

When I got back and told Uncle Martin, he said that maybe I could skate down to Wall Street and have lunch with him. He said it's downhill all the way.

FRIDAY, SEPTEMBER 9, 1938

Aunt Clara talked to me about school. I told her I didn't want to go. I don't want to be in a class with American girls who will make fun of me because I am a foreigner. I've seen the American girls in the park, and they don't look so nice.

She said she would think it over and that perhaps we could hire a tutor. I hadn't even thought of that. I would so much rather have a tutor than go to school.

SATURDAY, SEPTEMBER 10, 1938

The only thing that Uncle Martin doesn't like to do is sit still. If he isn't doing something he drums his fingers on the table, smokes his Camel cigarettes, makes smoke rings, and then pokes his finger through the rings before they evaporate.

It was raining hard all morning, and on rainy days

Uncle Martin photographs things he finds around the kitchen: silverware, glasses, cups, saucers, eggs, bread, onions, apples, pears, anything.

He places them on the kitchen table or the window ledge and spends hours deciding the exact right arrangement and the exact right place to stand. Finding where to stand is a big part of being a good photographer, Uncle Martin says.

He's very patient, also. He says if you're not patient, you shouldn't be a photographer.

The hallways are covered with his photographs. When I first saw them, I thought they were pretty ordinary. But now I realize they aren't. The way he photographs the ordinary things makes them seem extraordinary.

After he was finished in the kitchen he made me my first ice-cream soda. It's called a Black and White because it's made with chocolate syrup and vanilla ice cream. It should really be called a Brown and White.

SUNDAY, SEPTEMBER 11, 1938

Uncle Martin takes photographs of Aunt Clara without her knowing.

He takes one of his cameras, puts it on the big, low table in front of the living room couch, squats down on the floor, and pretends to be cleaning it.

Uncle Martin is forever cleaning his cameras, so there is nothing suspicious about this.

Then, when he calls Aunt Clara into the room and asks her some nonsensical questions, Aunt Clara gets this very sweet, quizzical look on her face, and Uncle Martin coughs while the camera clicks away.

MONDAY, SEPTEMBER 12, 1938

Mr. Allen invited me to visit.

As soon as I came, he insisted I go to the bathroom and wash my hands. I don't like the way his soap smells. It's called Ivory — I guess because of the color. It says IVORY right on the soap.

I told him I didn't want to disturb him, but he said he was stuck and my company was most welcome.

I asked him what he was stuck on, and he said the ending of the story he was writing.

It's about a blind girl and a man who fall in love and decide to get married right away. She invites her friends over because their romance has been so whirlwind, no one has had a chance to meet him. It's then that she finds out he's a Negro, which of course she didn't know because she was blind.

Mr. Allen said he's stuck because he doesn't know how it's going to end. I told him I didn't see how that could be since they are his characters and he's the writer, and so it could end however he wanted it to.

He said it doesn't always work out that way, and besides, he wasn't sure how he wanted it to end.

He asked me if I thought the man should have told the girl he was a Negro because she was blind and wouldn't know.

I never thought of that and I don't know what to think now. I wish I could have been more of a help, because Mr. Allen seemed genuinely perplexed.

The floor of his apartment is covered with crumpled-up sheets of yellow paper and little saucers of Coca-Cola. He said that the mice are eating his story at night, and he has been forced to defend himself. The mice are attracted by the sweet smell of the Coca-Cola. They drink too much of it and go away, and something about the bubbles makes their stomachs explode.

It's nice being in Mr. Allen's apartment because it's so quiet because of the soundproofing, but it's also a little strange.

WEDNESDAY, SEPTEMBER 14, 1938

Uncle Martin showed me where he hides the Hershey's bars. Aunt Clara *adores* Hershey's bars, and since she's on this diet she has forbidden Uncle Martin to let her find out where they are.

They're in the ice bucket on the top of the pantry cabinets. You need the little stepladder from the kitchen closet to get up high enough to reach in and get one, which frankly I think is a little silly. But Uncle Martin says that in the past, Aunt Clara has discovered his hiding places and eaten all the Hershey's bars, and he has "paid dearly for it."

THURSDAY, SEPTEMBER 15, 1938

For the first time I saw what Mr. Lippman does with his hearing aid. Mr. Esposito told me about it.

When someone Mr. Lippman doesn't like talks to him, he slides his hand inside his jacket and turns off his hearing aid. Then he just nods and smiles.

Mr. Esposito told me that Mr. Lippman's wife had to be sent "upstate" to a hospital because of her nerves. He seems much relieved, however, since he got a letter from his sister, who is safe in England now.

FRIDAY, SEPTEMBER 16, 1938

Mrs. Parrish doesn't speak very much because she has a bad stutter. Susie says she's quite embarrassed about it and does hours of exercises every day. Her room is right off the kitchen, next to Susie's, so sometimes you can hear her repeating over and over hard-to-say sentences: "I owned a wooden wheelbarrow." "Feed me the food in full view of the family." Sentences like that.

I try to be nice to her, but it's hard because she doesn't say much. She's from Ireland.

She said she's going to teach me to bake, but she had a lot of trouble saying "bake."

SATURDAY, SEPTEMBER 17, 1938

Uncle Martin won "Sober Sue," although I told him that what he did was completely against the rules.

He took me into the living room and told me to sit there with my hands covering my eyes until he gave the order.

I sat there for what seemed like a long time and didn't look until he said okay.

When I did look, he was standing right in front of me wearing Mrs. Parrish's uniform (Mrs. Parrish is a little chunky), even including her white cap and apron, and carrying a silver serving tray bearing a soup tureen, soup bowls, and wine glasses.

I had to admit it was one of the funniest things I've ever seen and I couldn't help but laugh out loud. The sound of my own laughter startled me.

It was the first time I had laughed in a long, long time.

MONDAY, SEPTEMBER 19, 1938

Susie took me to the Automat.

It's called an Automat because almost everything is automatic.

She gave me a dollar, and I went to the counter where the change lady takes it and gives you twenty nickels faster than you can imagine.

The Automat is prettier than the coffeehouses in Vienna. It's so light and airy, and the shiny marble walls are dotted with rows of glass windows. The glass windows are really little doors and behind each one is something good to eat: sandwiches, chicken potpies, desserts of all kinds.

When you put your nickel in the slot, the window opens and you take what's there. It's so much fun.

My favorite, though, is getting Susie's coffee. (She won't let me have my own, not even a little with my milk. I told her I had coffee all the time in Vienna, but Susie said, "Coffee is no good for little girls." I tried to explain to her that I am twelve and a half, far too old to be considered a little girl, but it didn't do me any good.)

When you pull the lever, the coffee comes gushing

out of a dolphin-head spout and fills the cup in an instant right to the top without spilling a drop.

Some people who go to the Automat are poor. Susie says they go there because they can get something to eat for nothing, although I don't see how what they eat can be very nourishing.

I watched this one lady who looked to be terribly ill and terribly dirty pour ketchup into a bowl of hot water, stir it up, and drink it like it was the most delicious tomato soup in the whole world.

The man she was with had taken a whole bowl of lemon wedges that they have where you get your tea and coffee. He was patiently squeezing each one into a glass, making sure he got every last drop, then he added lots of sugar, some water, and had himself a lemonade.

I saw one man put his nickel into the slot and take out a sandwich. But instead of closing the little door, he took a piece of chewing gum from his mouth and put it where the window was supposed to close, so that it stayed open.

Then he sat down, waited for the empty window to be filled, and got another sandwich.

WEDNESDAY, SEPTEMBER 21, 1938

I visited Mr. Allen again today. He wanted to know if I had an answer to his question yet, but I didn't, which didn't seem to surprise him.

He asked me if I had noticed the difference between the people who lived on the odd-numbered floors and those who lived on the even-numbered floors.

I admitted that I hadn't, and he said that was all right because I had only been here a short while.

The people on the even-numbered floors were intelligent, courteous, sophisticated, and friendly, while those on the odd-numbered floors were petty, narrow-minded, and "as boring as all get-out."

THURSDAY, SEPTEMBER 22, 1938

Uncle Martin asked me today if I had heard about the dull seaside town. It was so dull that one day the tide went out and never came back.

I heard another good American expression while listening to the radio with him tonight: "making whoopee."

He said I should come with him on Sundays when he

goes to the park to take photographs. He said Sunday mornings are the best. That's when everyone's still sleeping, the city is quiet, and you can have it all to yourself.

Sunday is the hardest day of the week for me, because it makes me think of Daddy, so I said yes.

SUNDAY, SEPTEMBER 25, 1938

One of Uncle Martin's cameras has a fake lens. It looks just like a regular camera, but it isn't. He made it himself.

The regular lens, the one in front, is a decoy so no one will suspect what he is really up to.

The real lens is on the side, and unless you were looking for it, you would never notice it.

We went to Central Park for what Uncle Martin calls some "chance portraits." He calls them that because he sits on a park bench and waits to see who will, by chance, come sit near him.

He likes to catch people when they're not hiding what they're thinking. "People without masks," he calls them.

It's eerie — you can almost read their minds because they are unaware that he is taking their picture.

Uncle Martin set up his tripod and camera, and we sat there feeding peanuts to the pigeons and waiting.

After a while a couple with their arms around each other sat down right near us. They looked like they were very much in love and were cherishing every minute they could spend together.

Uncle Martin winked, meaning he was ready. I did just as he instructed: I got up, fixed my hair, stood about ten feet in front of him, and smiled the biggest smile I could manage.

Uncle Martin had his head under the hood and appeared to be focusing on me when really he was looking right at the couple in the side lens. They never suspected a thing.

It was a good day. Uncle Martin took about twenty photographs, and he thinks one or two might turn out okay, but we'll have to see when he gets in the darkroom. Uncle Martin spends hours in his darkroom.

MONDAY, SEPTEMBER 26, 1938

Mr. Allen was waiting downstairs in the lobby this morning for his fried-egg sandwich to be delivered. That's what he has for breakfast every morning.

He was in such a good mood, I just had to ask him why. He said he was very close to a solution to his "dilemma." By "dilemma," I think he means the ending to his story. I asked him what the solution was, but he said he wasn't prepared to speak about it just yet.

WEDNESDAY, SEPTEMBER 28, 1938

Uncle Martin never misses his favorite radio shows: Jack Benny, Edgar Bergen, and especially his most favorite, Fred Allen.

He suggested that I listen to the radio with him because it might help with my vocabulary.

Frankly I think some of the comedians could use help with their own vocabularies.

I must admit he's right. I heard another good American word on the radio: "hog." It means to take everything for yourself and not leave any for anyone else.

I'm adding it to my list. So far I have:

Cooped-up
Tending to my business
Hiya, Toots
Swell
Baloney
Making whoopee

And now, hog. Pretty good, I think.

I wish Sophy were here — then we could have fun making a list of all these good American words. I could write to her, but I don't know where she is and she doesn't know where I am. Uncle Martin is trying his best, I know, but so far we haven't heard from anyone.

I'm glad Sophy is not in Vienna. Uncle Martin said she will be safe in England.

He showed me some of the photographs he developed in the darkroom. The one of the couple didn't come out very well, much to my surprise. But the one of the old lady who sat near us after they left was wonderful.

In Uncle Martin's photographs, people always come

out looking elegant and dignified, no matter what they're really like.

The old lady was poor, and her fingernails were dirty and bitten down. She was wearing a soiled raincoat, and boots that were falling apart. But in Uncle Martin's photograph, she looks like an empress.

SUNDAY, OCTOBER 2, 1938

There are stories in the newspaper about Hitler and Czechoslovakia. What will happen now? they ask. Uncle Martin hides the newspapers from me because he doesn't want me to worry, but I know where he puts them.

The newspapers say the same thing will happen in Czechoslovakia that happened in Vienna. They will talk. They will convince themselves that Hitler is not so terrible. And then there will be no Czechoslovakia, just like there is no Austria.

Everyone will stick their head in the sand, hoping Hitler will go away and leave them alone, just as Max said.

No one cares about anyone else as long as they are safe.

If Hitler came to America and marched down Fifth Avenue, the people on Central Park West wouldn't care as long as they were left alone.

MONDAY, OCTOBER 3, 1938

We took the double-decker bus all the way down Fifth Avenue to the Empire State Building.

I had my ten cents ready because the bus drivers don't like it if you hold up the line because it makes the buses late. Since all they're doing is going up and down Fifth Avenue all day, I don't see what the hurry is.

I sat on the top, but it was too cold for Susie.

Susie was walking very, very fast from the bus stop to the Empire State Building. She insisted we hold hands because there were so many people and she didn't want us to get separated. But she was pulling me so hard, my feet almost left the ground. When we got to the lobby I asked her why she was walking so fast. She said that sometimes, over the past few years, people in despair had thrown themselves off the top of the building and she didn't want to get hit!

We ate in a restaurant that's on the 86th floor. Then we went all the way up to the observation deck on the

102nd floor. We were so high up, we could see white clouds floating below us. You can see the cars whizzing around down there, but you can barely make out the people — they look like little bugs. And there is no sound — it's completely silent.

On the way home, I made Susie take me on the subway. Susie *hates* the subway. She said if I had to take the subway all the time like she does, I would hate it, too. But I don't and I don't.

The only thing I don't like is the itchy yellow straw seats, but I don't sit.

I stand and look out the window of the first car. It's right next to the tiny compartment where the man who drives the train sits, although you can't see in there. Sometimes I wonder what he looks like, and sometimes I even wonder if there's really anyone in there.

It's thrilling to look out as the train hurtles through the dark tunnel, the lights flashing red, green, orange, the wheels screaming on the curved steel tracks, the trains shaking from the speed.

I especially like the express train, which gets going really, really, fast because it doesn't have to stop at most of the stations. When it goes past, everyone standing on the platform is turned into one long blur.

It's more complicated riding the subways than the buses. There are so many different trains going to so many different places.

On the way home the front car was pretty deserted. A couple of men were napping and a lady was reading the newspaper, and there was plenty of room.

But when we got to Forty-second Street, it was a little after five o'clock and people going home from work flooded into the car and onto the train. Within seconds we were all crowded right up against each other. It got worse at every stop, and we were lucky to get out at our station.

When we got back, we went to Susie's room to get some candy.

"It's time you knew," she said, and somehow I knew she was going to tell me about Eva.

She lowered her head and spoke in a voice that said, "Don't say anything until I'm done." A voice I had never heard Susie use before.

Eva had a boyfriend whom Aunt Clara and Uncle Martin didn't like for many reasons, one being that he was too old: twenty-six, nine years older than Eva.

Eva promised she would stop seeing him, but Susie could tell that she didn't.

Then, one day, Eva confided to Susie that she was going to have a baby. Susie didn't know what to do but she knew she had to tell Aunt Clara.

Aunt Clara and Uncle Martin were shocked and saddened, and to complicate matters even further, Eva intended to have the baby even though the baby's father had disappeared.

They decided that the best thing to do was send her to Nantucket, to the hotel they went to every summer. She could rest there and have her baby in privacy. Susie went with her.

Then there were "complications." Susie started to cry when she said the word "complications." It took some time before she was able to go on.

Eva died giving birth to a premature baby who lived only five days.

Susie said no one had wanted to tell me about this when I first arrived because I had enough "sorrow on my mind."

We both sat there quietly until we heard Uncle Martin rummaging around in the kitchen, looking for something to eat.

I left Susie in her room after a while and went out to join Uncle Martin in the kitchen, acting as if everything was the same.

TUESDAY, OCTOBER 4, 1938

Uncle Martin said that after a while, Aunt Clara begins to act just like the character she is playing and not at all like her real self.

Sometimes it gets so bad, he has to read the script so he can learn who he's going to be married to while the play is running.

He bought me some bubble gum because I told him I wanted to learn how to blow bubbles like the girls I saw in Central Park.

I went right to my room. At first I wasn't doing very well, and I felt sure I must look foolish, so I went to the bathroom to see.

I didn't look nearly as awful as I feared, and I thought it might be a good idea to practice right there in front of the mirror.

It helped, and before long I was actually making bubbles. I wanted to see just how big a bubble I could make, but I went too close to the mirror and the bubble burst all over it and I had the most difficult time getting it off. I think there's still some on it.

WEDNESDAY, OCTOBER 5, 1938

Susie and I went to the movies today. It was cold and rainy, and we didn't want to stay inside all day.

She gave me twenty cents: fifteen cents so I could pay for my own ticket and a nickel for my popcorn.

Before the picture came on there was a newsreel showing Nazi soldiers marching and Hitler giving one of his speeches. I started to shake and had to leave.

Susie apologized all the way home, saying she didn't realize they would show newsreels, but it wasn't her fault.

I had another awful dream about Daddy. It was like the one I always have, only worse.

Daddy was at the foot of the bed, like before. He looked like he was standing closer to me — so close, I was tempted to touch him. Daddy wanted to speak to me, I could see, but I knew he wouldn't, and this time I didn't even hope.

But that wasn't all that was different. Mother wasn't

there, and a big yellow Jewish star was pinned to Daddy's coat. A yellow star just like the ones I saw people wearing in the newsreels.

He could see that I was staring at the star and he tried to tear it off, but it wouldn't come off and he started crying and the dream ended and I was awake and terrified.

THURSDAY, OCTOBER 6, 1938

Last night we had dinner at the Rainbow Room, which is at the top of one of the really tall skyscrapers (that's what they're called because the tops scrape the sky). There was a big window, and you could look out over the whole city. It was pretty scary, and I got dizzy.

SUNDAY, OCTOBER 9, 1938

Uncle Martin wanted to show me where he gets "proper" cheesecake. There's only one pastry shop that has it, but fortunately it wasn't too far away and so we walked there. Uncle Martin likes to walk, and so do I.

I've never seen a cheesecake that big. It covered the entire top of the glass counter. It had a shiny crisscross top, and was dotted with yellow raisins, just as Uncle Martin described.

Uncle Martin is also very specific about the exact *piece* of the cheesecake he wants.

He directed one of the bakery ladies (she knew Uncle Martin, because when he came in, she said to the other lady, "Here he comes again") to cut his piece from the middle, not the corner. Uncle Martin doesn't like to get it from the corner because then there's too much crust. "I'm interested in cheesecake, not crust," he said. "If I wanted crust, I would get apple pie."

The lady cut his piece, took some flattened cardboard from a pile, folded and tucked it until it became a cake box, and lined it with tissue paper she snatched from a nearby dispenser. Then she gently lifted up the piece of cheesecake and placed it in the box like she was putting a sleeping baby in her crib.

I told Uncle Martin he takes more time choosing a piece of cheesecake than he does choosing the subject for his photographs, and he looked at me sternly and said, "Is there something wrong with that?"

TUESDAY, OCTOBER II, 1938

The girl playing Wendy has quit. Her mother said that Mr. Robie has been too hard on her and she can no longer tolerate it.

They have to find someone to replace her right away, and Aunt Clara said she wants me to audition for the part, *tomorrow.*

I assumed she was joking, but she wasn't.

She said that I already know most of the lines (which isn't really true at all), and with my natural talent, she was sure I would get the part. I'm not even sure I *want* the part, but Aunt Clara was sure enough for both of us.

It's already three o'clock in the morning and I've been up all night going over Wendy's lines. The audition is at ten.

WEDNESDAY, OCTOBER 12, 1938

Just before I went out onto the stage, Aunt Clara pinched my cheeks so hard, I started to tear. She said it would put some color back in my face. I was a little nervous, and I imagine quite pale.

She reminded me to bite my lips really hard just before I began to speak, so they too looked rosy.

THURSDAY, OCTOBER 13, 1938

I got the part!

I'm going to play Wendy Darling, and Aunt Clara is going to play my mother!

The play is opening this Saturday night.

Aunt Clara does not want me to sit with the script for hours memorizing my lines. She thinks that's a big mistake. She wants me to read it through without even thinking about my lines. Just picture the play and imagine what it would be like to be Wendy.

Who is she?

What is she like?

How does she think?

What does she feel?

I must learn to *be* Wendy. She says "be" with great emphasis. The only way the part can be played properly is if I feel inside what Wendy is like.

She asked about Sophy, which startled me. Did I feel

comfortable with Sophy? I couldn't imagine what any of this had to do with the play.

Aunt Clara said that as soon as I felt as comfortable with Wendy as I did with Sophy, I could begin memorizing my lines — but not a moment before.

FRIDAY, OCTOBER 14, 1938

Aunt Clara took me to the theater. She wanted me to feel what it was like when it was empty.

We walked up and down the aisles, all around backstage (I saw my dressing room), and even onto the stage. Aunt Clara snapped her fingers in the air to show me what the sound was like.

It was strange being there. Strange because it didn't seem as unfamiliar as I thought it would. It felt comfortable, as if it wasn't my first time there. As if I had been there before.

SATURDAY, OCTOBER 15, 1938

I've never been so excited in my entire life! My name is in the *Playbill*! I'm putting it right here in my diary:

INTRODUCING, AS WENDY DARLING,
TEN-YEAR-OLD, VIENNA-BORN JULIE WEISS.

I showed Aunt Clara that they had gotten my age wrong, but she said it wasn't a mistake. They like you to be even younger than you are so your acting will seem even more astonishing.

I didn't forget any of my lines, which was truly a miracle. I was so nervous, I wanted to scream.

I told Uncle Martin that I didn't think I delivered any of my lines in a very convincing fashion, and he laughed and said I sounded just like my aunt.

All my friends from the building came: Mr. Esposito, Mrs. Lowenstein, Mr. Allen (it was quite a compliment that he came out), Mr. Smalls, and Susie.

Of course I didn't see any of them during the play, just later backstage, when everyone gathered in Aunt Clara's dressing room.

SUNDAY, OCTOBER 16, 1938

I slept till eleven o'clock. I threw a robe on as soon as I saw how late it was, and went out to the kitchen.

Aunt Clara and Uncle Martin were already up. The

newspapers were spread out all over the kitchen table. As soon as he saw me, Uncle Martin started reading out loud:

"'Julie Weiss is a promising young actress who appears to be as beautiful on the inside as she undeniably is on the outside.'"

Aunt Clara said that was *The New York Times,* which is the only newspaper that counts. But Uncle Martin said we should read more, even if they don't count.

One said my performance was "subtle beyond my years"; one that I was "radiant"; and another that I was "a new, natural young talent."

All the reviews were splendid.

Aunt Clara said that Mr. Garfinkel called to congratulate everyone on the reviews and he wanted to speak to me but she told him I was still sleeping.

When I went outside, "Red Mike" and "Black Mike" clapped, and Mr. Esposito asked for my autograph.

MONDAY, OCTOBER 17, 1938

Aunt Clara still doesn't like Mr. Buttinger. She says he's a hypochondriac and he's getting on her nerves.

Aunt Clara thinks he's always complaining about how ill he is just to call attention to himself.

He's been very nice to me, though. While we were playing one of our scenes together, he took me by the arm and turned me slightly toward the audience. When we were backstage later, he told me that was so they could see all of me.

Mr. Robie has been nice also. He walks just like a cat: slow, steady, cautious. He looks like a black cat because he always always wears black pants and a black turtleneck.

He keeps reminding me not to do too much. He says I'm doing very well but I should try not to *act* like Wendy but to *pretend* that I *am* Wendy.

I'm honestly not sure what the difference is.

TUESDAY, OCTOBER 18, 1938

Seeing how a play is put together behind the scenes is like seeing how a magician does his tricks, only it doesn't ruin the magic. It makes it more magical.

⊹ ⊹ ⊹

WEDNESDAY, OCTOBER 19, 1938

Another good thing about being in a play is that I definitely can't go to school.

Aunt Clara has hired a tutor for me. Her name is Miss Bliss, and she comes on Wednesdays and Mondays at four. (There's no play on Mondays, and only a matinee on Wednesdays and Sundays, but Miss Bliss can't come on Sundays.)

She teaches the sixth grade in a school right near here and has tutored child actors before, which was the first thing she told me. She said I speak English surprisingly well for someone so new to this country, and I told her about Miss Sachs, and about Ella Fitzgerald and how much I think listening to her singing has helped me.

Miss Bliss said that sounded like fun, but first we were going to review some fundamentals to see how much I knew and to make sure "our foundations are strong." Miss Bliss says "our" a lot when I think she means "your."

She doesn't strike me as the type of person who really says what she thinks. I don't think she really thought listening to Ella Fitzgerald was fun. I don't know why she said it, then. I've never understood people like Miss Bliss, and I don't think I ever will.

THURSDAY, OCTOBER 20, 1938

Acting is so exciting. It's the best game of make-believe I've ever played. I've never done anything like it before in my whole, entire life.

Knowing the audience is listening to my every word, laughing when I say something funny, holding their breath when I'm in danger. Hearing my own voice but knowing someone else is speaking. Someone who isn't me, but I'm them.

Being someone else night after night is the most incredible feeling. It is a blessing and a relief.

FRIDAY, OCTOBER 21, 1938

I was having trouble with one of my scenes. The one where the lost boys shoot me with an arrow when Peter brings me to be their mother.

I was certain Mr. Robie was going to say something, but he didn't. I wanted to ask him if I was doing it right, but Aunt Clara said not to. If you ask a director what they think, you will regret it for the rest of your career.

MONDAY, OCTOBER 24, 1938

I've decided to write down all the important things Aunt Clara says about becoming a great actress:

- Anything less than perfection is a compromise.
- Theories about good acting are far less important than good acting.
- Complete control at all times is essential.
- The outside must reflect the inside.
- On the stage a woman can be anything.
- Make-believe tears are for make-believe audiences.
- A true actress doesn't speak lines on command.

Aunt Clara takes acting very seriously.

TUESDAY, OCTOBER 25, 1938

Mrs. Delmar uses a rabbit's foot to blend my makeup. She also likes to have it around for good luck.

She's not the only one. A lot of people in the cast are superstitious. Mr. Buttinger doesn't allow any whistling while he's appearing in a play, and Margaret, who plays Peter, insists on coming in the door backward.

Mrs. Delmar said she would show me tomorrow how to take off my makeup using cold cream.

WEDNESDAY, OCTOBER 26, 1938

It's funny how some people aren't at all like their names. Mr. Smalls isn't small, and Miss Bliss is whatever the opposite of "bliss" is.

THURSDAY, OCTOBER 27, 1938

Mr. Buttinger got into trouble today because of his smoking. He insists on smoking backstage even though he knows it's not allowed.

The fireman caught him. He said he would let him off with a warning this time, but if he caught him again it would be "curtains." He winked when he said "curtains," which was very funny. But of course Mr. Buttinger didn't think it was funny at all. Mr. Buttinger doesn't have a very good sense of humor.

FRIDAY, OCTOBER 28, 1938

Aunt Clara said when I go to see *You Can't Take It With You* with Susie, I should listen to the way Spring Byington says her lines. That way, I can improve my speaking voice.

She also said I should brush my hair five hundred strokes a day, even though I wear a wig as Wendy.

- A successful actress must take care of her body.
- Never repeat lines like a trained parrot.
- An actress must become her character for the lines to sound natural.
- Smiling is not a God-given gift: It must be practiced.

Aunt Clara suggested I practice various expressions in front of the mirror to improve my range: happy, sad, lonely, surprised, confused, frightened. It's astonishing how easy it is for me to act frightened.

SUNDAY, OCTOBER 30, 1938

Mr. Robie has been spending a lot of time with me this past week. I was worried it was because of my accent, but it doesn't seem to be that. He said I have to learn to project my voice without shouting. He wants me to slow down my speech so I speak more dis-tinct-ly. He said it just like that.

Mr. Buttinger is so much like Mr. Darling. He's so absentminded that he came to the theater today with one brown shoe and one black.

I told Aunt Clara I was worried because everyone in the cast seems to be so much better than me, especially Margaret. But she said that playing with superior actors is the only way to learn.

MONDAY, OCTOBER 31, 1938

We had the most frightening evening last night.
Aunt Clara was having dinner with Mr. Garfinkel, and Uncle Martin was listening to the radio. I joined

him, expecting to hear Edgar Bergen and Charlie McCarthy, since it was Sunday night.

But Uncle Martin didn't like Edgar Bergen's guest, and so he turned the dial to a station that was playing boring dance music. Suddenly the music stopped, and there was a special bulletin.

It said that after some mysterious explosions on the planet Mars, a huge, flaming object had fallen from the sky and landed across the river in New Jersey. They were sending a mobile unit to the scene, and we were told we should stand by for further bulletins. Then the music came back on.

We stared at each other, too afraid to say anything because we might miss the bulletin.

Then a reporter at the scene said that the state police had roped off the area to keep back the spectators. He sounded agitated, and there was frantic shouting in the background. You could hear a strange hum, which he said was coming from the unidentified flying object.

Then, in a startled voice, he said that something was crawling out of the rocket ship. There was more than one, and they had black eyes, tentacles, and saliva dripping from their mouths. He sounded terrified, but continued to report.

The police were approaching them, holding a white flag of truce. Suddenly the horrible creatures began firing heat rays, which burned alive spectators and police alike. There were now forty dead, and martial law had been declared. Then the radio station lost contact with the mobile unit. And then, more music.

I was afraid it was worse than monsters from outer space. I was afraid Hitler and his Nazis had found a way to cross the ocean and were coming to attack the Jews in America.

Uncle Martin tried to call the restaurant where Aunt Clara was having dinner, but no one answered. He went over to the window and pulled back the curtains — just like Max did that night in Vienna when the Nazis in their trucks came, shouting, "Kill the Jews, kill the Jews."

I could hear Daddy on the phone with Mr. Heller, and feel Mother next to me on the couch. I turned to look at Mother, but there was no one there and then the door opened, just like it did that night, but this time it was Aunt Clara.

"Aunt Clara!" I cried, and ran to her and hugged her so tightly, I was afraid I might hurt her.

Uncle Martin told her what had happened, and she

laughed. She said there was nothing of the sort happening outside. It was such a nice night, she had decided to walk home after dinner.

She went to the telephone, laughing as she dialed, and spoke to someone she knew at *The New York Times*. He told her it was a hoax — some silly radio program, nothing more.

Mr. Esposito told me that Mrs. Lowenstein also had listened to the program and was going to swallow some poison so she could avoid the horrors of the Martian invasion from outer space. But first she had brought down her dogs for safekeeping, and Mr. Nicolson had convinced her that there wasn't any invasion.

WEDNESDAY, NOVEMBER 2, 1938

Margaret is still worried that her costume doesn't conceal all of her flying harness, and no matter how many times I assure her that it does, she continues to worry. She says if anyone in the audience sees it, it spoils the whole affect.

She comes early nearly every day to practice her flying, even though she doesn't really need to. Aunt Clara says Margaret is a dedicated and devoted actress. It's hard to believe she's twenty-five — she looks so much younger.

After *Peter Pan*, she's going to Los Angeles to be in a movie.

FRIDAY, NOVEMBER 11, 1938

It's so exciting coming out at night after the show is over. Thanks to the theater signs, it's light even though it's after ten.

There are always people waiting for Aunt Clara, Mr. Buttinger, and, of course, Margaret. But there are even some girls who are there to see me. They hold their autograph books out, and I sign them: Julie Weiss. It's nice being so popular.

SUNDAY, NOVEMBER 13, 1938

The radio says that the unspeakable is once again happening in Vienna. A desperate Jewish boy has killed a Nazi officer to avenge the death of his parents. Nazi mobs are running wild in the streets, looting and destroying Jewish shops and burning schools, hospitals, and synagogues to the ground.

The streets are littered with broken glass.

There are fires raging all over Vienna.

MONDAY, NOVEMBER 14, 1938

I write calmly, but I feel like screaming.

The Nazis are beating people in the streets of Vienna. They are rounding up Jews and taking them away.

Uncle Martin assures me he is making every effort to contact Daddy. He says I should be hopeful, but he looks hopeless.

And I am here. Safe and sound. Writing at my desk and sleeping in my warm bed while my father and brother are god knows where.

TUESDAY, NOVEMBER 15, 1938

After tonight's performance, Mr. Robie asked me to come back out on the stage. I was very, very nervous. I had felt distracted throughout the play, even though I had tried my hardest to concentrate.

I could see everyone creeping back into the wings, watching and waiting to see what he wanted to talk to me about. It was embarrassing.

He said I was not saying all my words clearly, and he wanted to work on it with me right then and there.

"Say apple," he said, and I said apple. "Again," he said, and I repeated it.

He wanted every person in the theater to hear each syllable.

"Say apple," he said, and I said apple. "Again," he said, and I repeated it, feeling foolish and thinking it sounded just fine the first time.

"You're losing the p-l-e," he said. I was so nervous and so aware of everyone watching that I didn't really even know what p-l-e he was talking about.

He must have seen that I didn't, because he said, "The p-l-e in apple. Now try it again."

"Apple," I said.

He raised his eyebrows as if to say, "You see, there it is," but I didn't. He started walking backward, keeping his eyes on me, and I thought for sure he was going to fall into the orchestra pit, but he landed on his feet, saying, as he did, "Again."

I said it louder this time, and with more emphasis. I wanted this all to end just as soon as possible.

"Again," he said, still walking backward up the

center aisle. I said it again, but he just kept saying again, again, and again until I could hardly see him.

He was all the way in the back of the theater, sitting in the very last row. "One last time," he said, and I was so angry and frustrated that I spit out, "AP-PLE," and as soon as I did, everyone in the wings burst into applause and I turned to see Aunt Clara beaming.

"Now," Mr. Robie said, "everyone can go home and get a good night's sleep."

WEDNESDAY, NOVEMBER 16, 1938

When I came in today, everyone in the cast had a shiny red apple for me as a present, which turned my face at least as red as the apples.

I am thankful I have the play to take my mind off everything else. Uncle Martin says there is still no news.

SUNDAY, NOVEMBER 20, 1938

We played a free matinee performance for orphans and poor children from around the city.

When the children entered the theater, a big bag of

candy was on every seat, with a balloon tied to the armrest. Mr. Garfinkel arranged it with Macy's, which is the big department store near here.

I could tell it was going to be a great performance from the opening act's first scene. Everyone sounded so much like their character and stayed that way the whole time.

Of course Margaret stole the show. Everyone in the audience held their breath as she flew over them, right up to the balcony.

She's completely fearless. It makes me nervous just to watch her.

When it was all over, the children leaped to their feet, clapped, yelled, and stomped up and down so much that the theater was shaking from the noise.

We had to take five curtain calls.

MONDAY, NOVEMBER 21, 1938

We went to dinner with Mr. and Mrs. Garfinkel.

Uncle Martin didn't want to go because he doesn't like to socialize, especially with "theater people."

But Aunt Clara put her foot down. Mr. Garfinkel said he had some special announcements to make and invited all of us, so Aunt Clara said she wanted the whole family to be together.

It was the first time Aunt Clara said we were a family.

It was a very pretty restaurant, and everyone was most attentive to Mr. Garfinkel. They hovered over him and made sure everything was just so.

He insisted we have caviar and champagne first. I liked the caviar — it tasted like salty bubbles.

Mrs. Garfinkel didn't stop talking for almost the whole dinner.

Mostly she talked about the new house they had just bought in Beverly Hills. Beverly Hills is in Los Angeles, where all the movie stars live. The Garfinkels have two homes now: an apartment in New York City, and the new house.

She explained that Mr. Garfinkel is going to produce movies half the year, and plays the other half.

She said if we came to visit we could stay with them because there was plenty of room. The house has a bowling alley, a billiard room, a music room (with a grand piano), a movie room (with its own projector, big screen, and seats, just like a real movie theater), a ten-car garage, horse stables, tennis courts, and two swimming pools — one for grown-ups and one for children.

"It's the land of milk and honey," Mrs. Garfinkel said, lifting her champagne glass, which had pink lipstick smeared on it.

Fortunately by the end of dinner she had run out of steam. (Uncle Martin whispered in my ear that she was "stewed to the gills.")

Mr. Garfinkel asked Aunt Clara if she ever thought about the movies. Aunt Clara looked surprised and said she hadn't, and Mr. Garfinkel said she'd better start.

Then he announced that he was going to produce a new play, called *Our Town*. It was "destined to become one of the great plays in the history of the American theater."

It's about two ordinary families growing up in a small town called Grover's Corners.

Mr. Garfinkel wants Aunt Clara and me to play mother and daughter again, just like we did in *Peter Pan*. He said he thinks we can bring "something special" to it.

I was very excited, but Aunt Clara was cool — she

can be like that if it's something important, like a new play.

She told Mr. Garfinkel that if he sent the script over in the morning, she would give him her answer by evening.

I so hope Aunt Clara will say yes, because the timing couldn't be more perfect. *Peter Pan* is closing Friday, and Mr. Garfinkel said we could begin rehearsals for *Our Town* as soon as Aunt Clara wants.

TUESDAY, NOVEMBER 22, 1938

Mr. Esposito brought the script up as soon as the messenger arrived.

Aunt Clara and I read it sitting side by side on the couch in the sunroom. I think we were both shaken when we read what happens to Emily, the character I am to play.

Emily dies giving birth, just like Eva. I didn't know what to do, so I just reached out and held Aunt Clara's trembling hand.

She turned to me. I had never seen her look so serious before. "Should we do it, and can we do it?" she asked.

I didn't hesitate for a moment. I told her that we could.

WEDNESDAY, NOVEMBER 23, 1938

Aunt Clara called Mr. Garfinkel and said yes. She told him it was a miraculous and deeply moving play and that we would be honored to play Mrs. Webb and her daughter, Emily.

Rehearsals start in two weeks, so that we can open Christmas Day. Aunt Clara and I aren't going to wait, though. We're going to begin our own rehearsals right here in the apartment, just as soon as *Peter Pan* closes.

THURSDAY, NOVEMBER 24, 1938

Mrs. Parrish may not know how to bake a proper cheesecake, but she certainly knows how to cook a proper turkey.

Uncle Martin showed me how to split the wishbone with him. He told me to make a wish, and I'm afraid I took longer to make a wish than he had counted on, but I wanted to really think about it.

I wished I could talk to someone in my family, just once.

FRIDAY, NOVEMBER 25, 1938

Tonight was the last performance.

The audience threw flowers until the stage was covered, and cried "Bravo!" until we left.

SATURDAY, NOVEMBER 26, 1938

Our Town is so poetic. Each time I read it, I think something different. One time I think how terribly terrifying life is, and another time I think how glorious it is.

Emily has the most eloquent lines, and she's perfect for me, or rather, I'm perfect for her. She's dreamy, just like me, and a little too smart for her own good. (She's the smartest student in her class, also.)

And the best part is that Emily is the best part: She's the star!

MONDAY, NOVEMBER 28, 1938

Aunt Clara had Mrs. Parrish serve lunch in the sunroom so we wouldn't have to stop rehearsing.

I don't know what came over me. I wasn't planning to say anything. I didn't even realize I had been thinking about it, although I must have. It was out of my mouth before I knew it.

I asked Aunt Clara why she and Mother didn't speak.

Aunt Clara can look any way she wants, so I knew the way she was looking at me was no accident.

"Do you really want to know?" she was saying.

"Yes," I said out loud.

"I see you're not only a good actress but a good audience," Aunt Clara said. "All right, then, I'll tell you."

It was Daddy.

Aunt Clara had met him first, before Mother. He saw her in a play in Vienna, came backstage, and they fell in love. At least Aunt Clara thought they had fallen in love.

She introduced Daddy to her family and was pleased that everyone liked him.

Unfortunately she was busy with the play and wasn't able to spend as much time with him as she would have liked.

Then, about a month after they first met, her friends told her they had seen her sister with Daddy almost every night for the past two weeks.

Aunt Clara confronted her with this, and she denied everything. But the next day Mother and Daddy eloped.

When the newlyweds returned to Vienna, Aunt Clara tried to reconcile herself with the situation, but she was unable to. She said that if it hadn't been for Uncle Martin, she wouldn't have survived. It was he who suggested they move to America.

I think right then my whole world changed, yet again. In an instant, I didn't even feel like myself. I felt like someone else, and I felt like *being* someone else. I wanted to return to Emily, to the scene we were working on.

It was the scene in the final act. The one in the cemetery. Emily is allowed to relive one day of her life, and she chooses her twelfth birthday. My last birthday with my family.

Emily's sentiments are so true, so simple, and so sweet — I wish I could grab them and hold them to me so I could have them for all time.

She sees herself and her family back then and realizes how little they all appreciated the preciousness of living each day.

She is saddened to see how little time we take to appreciate the simple joy of being alive. How we lose each moment in our concern for the next moment.

Anguished, she breaks down sobbing, and says:

. . . I can't look at everything hard enough. . . .

I can't. I can't go on. It goes so fast. We don't have time to look at one another.

I didn't realize. So all that was going on and we never noticed. . . .

Oh, earth, you're too wonderful for anybody to realize you.

Do any human beings ever realize life while they live it? — every, every minute? . . .

EPILOGUE

There is, regrettably, no documentary evidence available on the fate of Julie Weiss's uncle Daniel, or her friend Sophy's parents.

Mr. and Mrs. Heller are known to have been among the thousands of Viennese Jews transported to Dachau, the Nazi concentration camp, in early November 1938 during or after what became known as the Night of Broken Glass. They both perished there.

Martin and Clara Singer, along with Julie Weiss, moved to Los Angeles, California, in 1939. Clara made one film with Mr. Garfinkel, and although it was a critical and commercial success, she returned to the stage and never appeared in a film again.

Martin Singer died of lung cancer in 1941, the same year Susie Cooper married Mr. Smalls ("Black Mike") and Julie learned of her father's death.

Dr. Benjamin Weiss was attending a patient in the hospital two weeks after his daughter had arrived safely in America. Nazi soldiers, for reasons that are not known, ordered him to leave and, when he refused, shot him where he was standing.

This information was conveyed to Julie by Ruth Sachs, her former English teacher. Miss Sachs, who came to America in October 1938, happened to see Julie in the Los Angeles production of *Our Town.* She went backstage to speak to her, and they remained close friends for the rest of their lives.

With Ruth Sachs's help, Julie was able to find Sophy Marcus, who was still living in England, and Julie's brother, Max, who was in Palestine.

Max had been given a precious permit to emigrate to Palestine by a man unwilling to leave his critically ill older sister who had raised him.

Contact between Max and Julie was established in 1947, and in 1954, Max, accompanied by his wife and eight-year-old son, visited Julie in Los Angeles.

Although Julie never married, in 1946 she had a child, Liesl. She also had a long and successful acting career. Like her aunt, who adopted her, she, too, chose to appear only on the stage.

LIFE IN EUROPE AND AMERICA IN 1938

HISTORICAL NOTE

Vienna was a cosmopolitan metropolis at the onset of World War II. It was also the home of almost all of the Jews in Austria. The Jewish people had considerable influence on Vienna's political, cultural, and economic life. In fact, a good deal of Austrian industry was owned by Jews, as were most of Vienna's liberal newspapers. The social composition of the Jewish community ranged from powerful bankers and industrialists to impoverished peddlers who had moved to town in large numbers before World War I. Most Jews were more liberal than the rest of the population, which intensified the already strong anti-Semitism in the country. Other Jews, however, adopted conservative political values, and even rejected their Judaism in order to assimilate themselves into the Austrian mainstream.

While anti-Semitism was always prevalent in Austria, it was not until Hitler annexed Austria into his

Reich that it became a truly unbearable place for the Jews. Indeed, Hitler rose to power in Germany with the intention of expanding his power throughout Europe. While he had economic and industrial plans for Europe (and, ultimately, for the world), his first, and most obscene, priority was to preserve what he deemed the perfect race of people — the "Aryan" race. To do this, he had to "weed out" those people who did not fit his picture of perfection. Many people were targeted, but it was the Jewish people who became Hitler's greatest enemy. He blamed the Jews for Germany's weakened economy, and for all of Europe's woes. He would stop at nothing to rid Europe of Jews once and for all.

Prior to his rise to power, in fact, Hitler mapped out what would become the bible of the Nazi movement, *Mein Kampf*, or *My Struggle*. In this text, Hitler expresses his dedication to the purity of the German race along with an irrational hatred for the Jews, who he claimed undermined German purity. And while many ignored or gave only a passing glance to these ranting words, they would become the blueprint for Hitler's domination of Europe and the destruction of European Jewry.

Since Hitler saw the Jews as nonhuman, they were segregated under his rule. The Nazis described the Jews as parasites and viruses, even as rats, in order to rally the so-called Aryan people against them. The Nazis sought to convince people that Jews would corrode their society and culture. Hitler's theory was that human survival depended on the eradication of the Jewish people. To this end, the phrase *Sieg Heil* came to be the salute of the Nazi movement. It means "Hail to Victory" — victory of light over dark, good over evil, Aryan over Jew.

When Hitler decided to create an *Anschluss* (union) with Austria, the Austrian government and its people were in a panic. The *Anschluss* threatened Austrian independence after all. When the vote that might have kept Austria's Chancellor Schuschnigg in control was forgone, Hitler's invasion of this civilized country was imminent. On March 13, 1938, Hitler and his troops marched into Austria. By a combination of threats and propaganda, the Nazis annexed Austria.

The most striking and disturbing outcome of Hitler's sudden and somewhat unopposed takeover of Austria was the way in which friends and neighbors turned so fiercely on one another. Where Jews and Gentiles once lived in peace as business partners and classmates, dining companions and playmates, overnight an angry rift divided them. Because the people of Austria took so quickly to Hitler's propaganda, what had taken years to accomplish in Germany took only the course of a few months to achieve in Austria. Persecution of the Jews began almost immediately. The Nazi anti-Semitic legislation, barring the Jews from their professions, from attending government schools and universities, and from marrying Gentiles, were very rapidly introduced. Most Jewish communal organizations were shut down. There was also considerable anti-Jewish violence as many Austrians reacted strangely enthusiastically to the Nazi takeover and the persecution of the Jews.

The degradation in Austria was miserable — Jewish shops were robbed, the shopkeepers beaten, and arbitrary arrests began. Jewish men and women were forced to clean the pavement on their knees with a strong solution of water and boric acid while crowds stood by and cheered. Now, the anti-Jewish attacks were even more extreme in Austria than they were in Germany.

Then, on the night of November 9, 1938, a massive,

coordinated attack on Jews throughout the German Reich proved just how far the hatred had already gone. That night has come to be known as *Kristallnacht*, or the Night of Broken Glass. The attack came after Herschel Grynszpan, a seventeen-year-old Jew living in Paris, shot and killed a member of the German Embassy staff there. He was angry at the treatment he and his family received from the Nazis when they, along with 15,000 other Jews, were expelled from Germany and transported by train to the Polish border. For Adolf Hitler, the shooting provided an opportunity to incite Germans to "rise in bloody vengeance against the Jews."

Mob violence broke out as the regular German police stood by and crowds of spectators watched. Nazi storm troopers along with members of the SS and Hitler Youth beat and murdered Jews, broke into and wrecked Jewish homes, and brutalized Jewish women and children.

All over Germany, Austria, and other Nazi-controlled areas, Jewish shops and department stores had their windows smashed and contents destroyed. Synagogues were especially targeted for vandalism, including desecration of sacred Torah scrolls. Hundreds of synagogues were systematically burned while local fire departments stood by. About 25,000 Jewish men were rounded up and later sent to concentration camps where they were often brutalized by SS guards and, in some cases, randomly chosen to be beaten to death.

In Germany, some of the top Nazi leaders held a meeting about the damage, and to discuss further measures to be taken against the Jews. One officer reported 7,500 businesses destroyed, 267 synagogues burned (with 177 totally destroyed), and 91 Jews killed. At this meeting the Nazis decided to eliminate Jews entirely from economic life in the Reich by transferring all Jewish property and enterprises to Aryans.

This was a pivotal moment. No one really knew how horrific it would get, but many Jews understood that they should leave Europe right away. The Zionist movement was becoming more active at this time. Zionists believed that a Jewish state should be established in Palestine, modern-day Israel. With a tremendous amount of effort from the Jewish Agency for Palestine, more than 44,000 German and Austrian Jews immigrated to Palestine by 1938. Beginning in May of 1938, the Jews began to work toward a Jewish exodus. Possibly half the community, which had numbered

176,000 in 1936, succeeded in finding refuge. In 1948, the United Nations established a Jewish homeland in British-controlled Palestine, which became the republic of Israel.

Emigration was difficult for Jews because of anti-Semitism throughout the world. Despite that fact, thousands of Jews immigrated to Palestine, to Britain, to North and South America, and to Shanghai. People within the United States thought there should be no interference from the U.S. in Germany's internal policies. Against the wishes of many Americans, however, 32,753 people from Germany had been admitted to the United States by the end of 1939, 80 to 85 percent of whom were Jews. The United States closed its gates to immigrants in 1940. Many relatives did not find out the fate of their loved ones until after the war. In the second half of 1941, Nazi deportation of the remaining Jews began. Almost all perished in the concentration camps of Terezin or Auschwitz. When Vienna was finally liberated in December of 1944, only 5,800 Jews (roughly 3 percent of the 1938 Jewish population) were still living there. Before the Holocaust, 9,797,000 Jews lived and prospered throughout Europe — less than half survived.

VIENNA, AUSTRIA
1938

Kärtnerstrasse is a popular shopping street in Vienna. Before Hitler's occupation of Austria, it was a favorite place of the upper class, among them many Jews, to shop and dine.

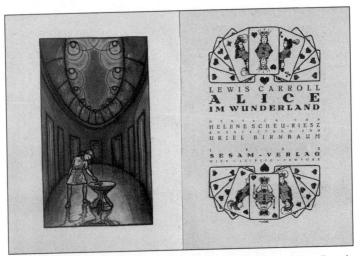

Written in 1865 by Lewis Carroll, Alice in Wonderland *was originally published in England, but was available throughout Europe. The story is about what the world looks like through the eyes of a child. Here is the frontispiece and title page from a German-language edition.*

Jews in Vienna were generally part of upper-middle class society as they were often professionals, scholars, or successful merchants. The parlor of this wealthy Jewish home reflects their privileged lifestyle.

Austrian Jews often socialized in cafés in Vienna discussing social, economic, and political issues of the day.

The Nazi reign in Germany began with somewhat subtle movements toward the "cleansing" of German society. Here, books and articles deemed "un-German" are collected by Nazi students.

Nazis burn "un-German" materials in a bonfire in Berlin in front of a large crowd.

Adolf Hitler entered the city of Vienna in March, 1938, as part of his plan to expand Nazi ideology and rule beyond Germany's borders. His arrival by motorcade was a dramatic moment for Vienna.

On the same day, Hitler addressed the crowds from the balcony of the Hofburg in Vienna. A native Austrian, Hitler was greeted with much enthusiasm by the people of Vienna.

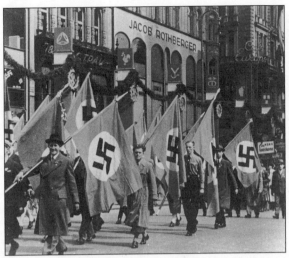

The Nazi flag was characterized by the swastika, an ancient symbol confiscated by the Nazis, that has come to symbolize the kind of hate that spawned the Nazi reign of terror, and ultimately, the Holocaust. Here, Nazi flags are carried in a May Day celebration parade in Vienna, 1938.

In order to effectively ostracize Jews from European society, Hitler began by forcing Jews to wear a yellow badge of the Star of David with Jude, the German word for "Jew," written on it.

Nazi soldiers were under the strict scrutiny of the very stern and demanding Hitler. He expected them to embody the ultimate perfection of the Aryan race. He inspired them with the salute Sieg Heil, *or "Hail to Victory." Here, he reviews his soldiers.*

Zionism, the movement that sought a Jewish homeland in Palestine, was in full force in Vienna under the young leadership of activists like Aron Meczer, pictured here (front, middle) with leaders of various youth movements. Aron Meczer sacrificed his life so that Jewish youth could escape safely from Nazi Austria to Palestine, which is now Israel.

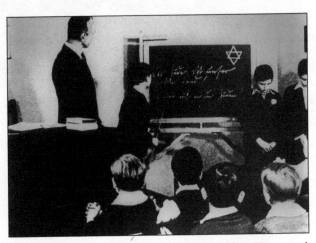

The degradation of Jews became a part of everyday life in Vienna under the Nazi reign. Here, Jewish students are humiliated in front of their classmates. Written on the blackboard are the words, "The Jew is our greatest enemy."

A crowd of Viennese children looks on as a Jewish boy is forced by Austrian Nazis to paint the word Jude on his father's store in order to identify it as a Jewish-owned shop. It was both emotionally and financially devastating for Jewish professionals and shopkeepers to be so willfully abandoned by long-time customers and friends.

A Viennese Jew is forced to scrub anti-Hitler slogans from the street in front of a crowd. These humiliating moments stripped Jews of their dignity.

Ultimately, most Jews were deported to concentration camps where they were tortured and murdered at the hands of Nazis. Here, Jews arrive at Auschwitz, one of the most horrible death camps in Europe.

Even though emigration was virtually impossible, many managed to get the necessary visas to leave. Jews lined up at the emigration office in Vienna hoping to escape.

NEW YORK, NEW YORK
1938

Some Jews were lucky enough to make it to America, where many settled in New York City, the port of entry for all immigrants from Europe. A booming metropolis, New York City is filled with famous shopping streets like Fifth Avenue, pictured here in 1939.

A landscaped park that runs from 59th Street to 110th Street in Manhattan, Central Park is an urban wonder. Developed in 1858, it was the first major American park intended entirely for public use.

In 1938, the radio was the main source of news and entertainment programming. Families regularly gathered around to listen to the day's events or to tune in to their favorite programs.

Times Square marks the center of the theater district. Above, the lights of Broadway have immortalized the stars and shows on the marquees that line this famous street. Below, *people arrive at a Broadway theater in droves.*

To be in a Broadway show is to achieve the ultimate goal of actors everywhere. It is a grueling process for the talented players who have performed on Broadway's many stages. Above, *actors audition for coveted roles in a play in 1940. Below, they rehearse.*

JED HARRIS
presents

OUR TOWN

A PLAY BY
THORNTON WILDER
with

FRANK CRAVEN

MOROSCO THEATRE

Written in 1937 by Thornton Wilder, Our Town *has become an American classic, famous for its wise and deeply human story of life in small-town America.* Our Town *premiered in New York City at the Morosco Theater.*

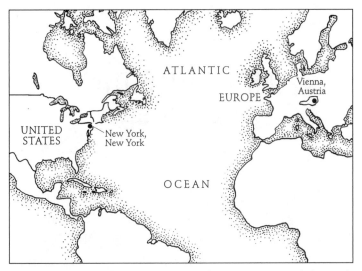

This map shows the approximate locations of Vienna, Austria, and New York, New York.

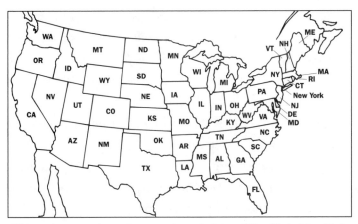

This modern map shows the approximate location of New York, New York.

ABOUT THE AUTHOR

Barry Denenberg is the author of several critically-acclaimed books for young readers, including two books in the Dear America series, *When Will This Cruel War Be Over?: The Civil War Diary of Emma Simpson,* which was named an NCSS Notable Children's Trade Book in the Field of Social Studies and a YALSA Quick Pick; and *So Far from Home: The Diary of Mary Driscoll, an Irish Mill Girl,* and two books in the My Name Is America series, *The Journal of William Thomas Emerson: A Revolutionary War Patriot,* and *The Journal of Ben Uchida, Citizen 13559, Mirror Lake Internment Camp.* Praised for his meticulous research, Barry Denenberg has written books about diverse times in American history, from the Civil War to Vietnam.

Barry Denenberg says, "Researching and writing *One Eye Laughing, The Other Weeping* was a particularly rewarding and gratifying experience.

"The Vienna of 1938 was a society that was fundamentally destroyed — certainly as far as Jews were concerned — when Hitler seized the city.

"Of course the magic of the Dear America books is that they are not about Adolf Hitler, but about Julie Weiss. To write her story, I needed to understand what it was like to have your entire world suddenly shattered. Researching Part One of the book was an extremely sad time for me, but necessary, if Julie and her family and friends were to emerge as real characters.

"Researching Part Two was a wholly different experience. In Part One, my research was straightforward: Austria, Vienna, and in particular Jewish life in 1930s Vienna.

"To write the second part, my research had to be less focused and more eclectic. The research seemed to take on a life of its own, as did the writing.

"Julie and her new life evolved in a way that felt beyond my control. Sentences flowed and daily entries fell into place in the most unpredictable and eerie fashion — as if I were directing a play that had already been written.

"The book ends on a note that seemed predestined. It was an astonishing experience, and I hope for you, the reader, it will be equally compelling.

"One last thing: When I was twelve, I read *Anne Frank: The Diary of a Young Girl.* Every year I re-read it, along with more current books and documentaries. The true beauty of Anne Frank's diary is that she always sounds so incredibly real. Her diary makes the Holocaust personal, not political; individual, not anonymous.

"I wrote Julie Weiss's diary with Anne Frank's near me at all times so I wouldn't forget, truly, what I was doing. It was a constant source of inspiration."

Denenberg's nonfiction works include *An American Hero: The True Story of Charles A. Lindbergh,* which was named an ALA Best Book for Young Adults, and a New York Public Library Book for the Teen Age; and *Voices from Vietnam,* an ALA Best Book for Young Adults, a *Booklist* Editors' Choice, and a New York Public Library Book for the Teen Age. He lives with his wife and their daughter in Westchester County, New York.

DEDICATION

I'll never write a book good enough for Jean,

so this will have to do.

ACKNOWLEDGMENTS

The author would like to thank Amy Griffin for her sensitive editorial work, and Chris Kearin and his fellow "book people" for their help.

Grateful acknowledgment is made for permission to reprint the following:

Cover portrait: Photograph of Liesl Joseph-Loeb, from *Voyage of the Damned,* by Gordon Thomas.
Cover background: Nazi soldiers marching, Ullstein Bilderdienst, Berlin.
Page 2: Hofburg Gate, Tony Frenkl Collection of the Austrian Heritage Collection, Courtesy of the Leo Baeck Institute, New York.
Pages 8, 114–115: "Gott Spricht zu jedem… /God Speaks to Each of Us," from *Rilke's Book of Hours: Love Poems to God* by Rainer Maria Rilke, translated by Anita Barrows and Joanna Macy. Copyright © 1996 by Anita Burrows and Joanna Macy. Used by permission of Putnam Berkley, a division of Penguin Putnam Inc.
Page 74: "Someone to Watch Over Me" copyright © 1926 by George and Ira Gershwin. All rights reserved. Used by permission of WARNER BROTHERS PUBLICATIONS U.S. Inc., Miami, Florida 33014.
Page 122: Central Park, Corbis-Bettman.
Page 224 (top): Kartnersträsse, FPG International, New York.

Page 224 (bottom): Alice im Wunderland, photograph © Fritz Simak, Meidlinger Hauptstraße.

Page 225 (top): Parlor in Jewish home, Leo Baeck Institute, New York.

Page 225 (bottom): Austrian Jews socialize in lounge, 1930. Museen der Stadt Wien, Austria/United States Holocaust Memorial Museum.

Page 226: Nazi students collect books, 1933. Ullstein Bilderdienst, Berlin.

Page 227: Nazis burn books, 1933. Ullstein Bilderdienst, Berlin.

Page 228: Hitler's motorcade, 1938. Imperial War Museum/Archive Photos.

Page 229: Hitler's speech at Hofburg in Vienna, 1938. Ullstein Bilderdienst, Berlin.

Page 230 (top): May Day march, Vienna, 1938. Library of Congress.

Page 230 (bottom): Girls with Star of David patches in Vienna, 1941. Oesterreichische Gesellschaft fuer Zeitgeschichte/United States Holocaust Memorial Museum.

Page 231: Hitler reviewing soldiers. Wide World Photo.

Page 232 (top): Aron Meczer and other youth leaders in Vienna, 1940. Courtesy Jacob Metzer.

Page 232 (bottom): Jewish students are humiliated in front of classmates, 1938. Institute of Contemporary History and Wiener Library, Ltd., London/United States Holocaust Memorial Museum. Neg. 02748.

Page 233: Jewish youth forced to paint "Jude" on father's store, 1938. Oesterreichische Gesellschaft fuer Zeitgeschichte/United States Holocaust Memorial Museum.

Page 234 (top): Viennese Jews scrub slogans from the streets. Dokumentationsarchiv des Oesterreichischen Widerstandes, courtesy of USHMM Photo Archives.

Page 234 (bottom): Arrival of deportees at Auschwitz. Brown Brothers, Sterling, Pennsylvania.

Page 235: Jewish Emigration, Vienna 1938–1939. Oesterreichische

Gesellschaft fuer Zeitgeschichte/United States Holocaust Memorial Museum.

Page 237: Fifth Avenue, New York City, c. 1939. Culver Pictures, New York.

Page 238: Central Park, New York City. Ewing Galloway.

Page 239: Family listening to radio. FPG International, New York.

Page 240 (top): Times Square, New York City. Ewing Galloway.

Page 240 (bottom): Broadway, New York City, c. 1930. Ewing Galloway.

Page 241 (top): Backstage tryouts, 1940. Culver Pictures.

Page 241 (bottom): Backstage rehearsal. Culver Pictures.

Page 242: Poster for *Our Town*. Museum of the City of New York Theatre Collection.

Page 243: Maps by Heather Saunders.

OTHER BOOKS IN THE DEAR AMERICA SERIES

A Journey to the New World
The Diary of Remember Patience Whipple
by Kathryn Lasky

The Winter of Red Snow
The Revolutionary War Diary of Abigail Jane Stewart
by Kristiana Gregory

When Will This Cruel War Be Over?
The Civil War Diary of Emma Simpson
by Barry Denenberg

A Picture of Freedom
The Diary of Clotee, A Slave Girl
by Patricia McKissack

Across the Wide and Lonesome Prairie
The Oregon Trail Diary of Hattie Campbell
by Kristiana Gregory

So Far from Home
The Diary of Mary Driscoll, an Irish Mill Girl
by Barry Denenberg

I Thought My Soul Would Rise and Fly
The Diary of Patsy, a Freed Girl
by Joyce Hansen

A Light in the Storm
The Civil War Diary of Amelia Martin
by Karen Hesse

A Coal Miner's Bride
The Diary of Anetka Kaminska
by Susan Campbell Bartoletti

Color Me Dark
The Diary of Nellie Lee Love
by Patricia McKissack

My Secret War
The World War II Diary of Madeline Beck
by Mary Pope Osborne

Library of Congress Cataloging-in-Publication Data
Denenberg, Barry.
One eye laughing, the other weeping: the diary of Julie Weiss / by Barry
Denenberg. — 1st ed.
p. cm. — (Dear America)
Summary: During the Nazi persecution of the Jews in Austria,
twelve-year-old Julie escapes to America to live with her relatives in
New York City.
ISBN 0-439-09518-2
1. Holocaust, Jewish (1939–1945) — Austria — Juvenile fiction. [1.
Holocaust, Jewish (1939–1945) Austria — Fiction.   2. Jews — Austria —
Fiction.   3. Austria — History — 1938–1945.   4. Emigration and immi-
gration — Fiction.   5. Diaries — Fiction.] I. Title. II. Series.
PZ7.D4135 On 2000
[Fic] — dc21   00-021920

CIP
10 9 8 7 6 5 4 3 2 1   0/0 01 02 03 04

The display type was set in Willow.
The text type was set in Stempel Schneidler.
Book design by Elizabeth B. Parisi
Photo research by Zoe Moffitt and Gabriela and Fritz Simak, Vienna.

Printed in the U.S.A. 23
First edition, October 2000